Molière's Plays

Translated by Curtis Hidden Page

Les Femmes Savantes
(The Learned Ladies)

Tartuffe
(The Hypocrite)

Le Bourgeois Gentilhomme
(The Tradesman Turned Gentleman)

Les Précieuses Ridicules
(The Affected Misses)

Le Médecin malgrè Lui
(The Doctor by Compulsion)

G. P. Putnam's Sons, Publishers

Les Précieuses Ridicules
(The Affected Misses)

Le Médecin Malgré Lui
(The Doctor by Compulsion)

By

Molière

Translated by

Curtis Hidden Page

Late Professor of Romance Languages and Literatures in Columbia University

G. P. Putnam's Sons
New York and London
The Knickerbocker Press
1912

The Knickerbocker Press, New York

LES
PRECIEUSES RIDICULES

COMÉDIE EN UN ACTE

18 NOVEMBRE, 1659

THE AFFECTED MISSES

OR

THE LUDICROUS LADIES OF
CULTURE

A COMEDY IN ONE ACT

NOVEMBER 18, 1659

(*The original is in prose*)

INTRODUCTORY NOTE

THE *Précieuses ridicules* marks the beginning of Molière's career as a dramatist. It was almost certainly written at Paris during the first year after his return there, and was the first new play given after the establishment of his troupe under the patronage of the king's brother. It was also the first in which he abandoned the close imitation of Italian models and drew his material from observation of the life about him; and it was the one in which he began the series of attacks upon affectation, snobbishness, and sham of every kind, that filled the rest of his life.

The word *précieuse* cannot be translated; but the phrase "lady of culture" is a fair equivalent for it, in both its good and its bad meanings. This "culture" which the *précieuse* of the seventeenth century represented, had, as is usual with conscious culture-movements, been at first a valuable and much-needed reform; it had, however, been overdone and artificialised, it had been made a cult and a fad; the fad had been taken up everywhere, by unintelligent and snobbish imitators; and a healthy reaction, in favour of common-sense and even coarseness, was long overdue. Molière made this reaction triumph. More than thirty years later Boileau, in his *Tenth Satire*, speaks of

> A *précieuse*—the last
> Of those once famous wits whom Molière
> With one sure stroke of art discredited.

3

The *précieux* movement had begun fully fifty years before Molière's comedy appeared. In its latest and degenerate stage, when he attacked it, its chief characteristics were refinement, tending to artificiality, of language; attention to the minor trifles and to the small-talk of literature; and a style of social intercourse and of love-making for which the novels of Mlle. de Scudéry furnished the model. It is from these novels, especially *Clélie* and *Artamène*, or *Le Grand Cyrus*, that the Madelon of the play has taken her conception of the proper conduct of a love-affair, which she expounds to the great amazement of her worthy father (p. 15). In each of them the necessary dénouement is delayed through ten long volumes, and there is plenty of time for the " adventures . . . jealousies, complainings, despairs, abductions, and the rest," which Madelon so much desires. In *Le Grand Cyrus*, for instance, the heroine Mandane suffers abduction four times, not to count four unsuccessful attempts. Most of the time, however, is spent in conversation, and especially in the discussion of minor problems of love and in parlour comment upon literature. The " Map of Love's Land," by which Cathos wishes her admirers to be guided, is given in Volume I. of *Clélie*. It shows the three rivers, Esteem, Gratitude, and Inclination, on which are situated the three cities of Love: Love-on-Esteem, etc. Starting from New-Acquaintance, one may float easily down the river Inclination to Love-on-Inclination; but as the current becomes swifter one is more than likely to be carried past the town and be lost in the Dangerous Sea beyond. It is far better, though more difficult, to go across country, by way of Wit, Familiar-Verse, Polite-Epistles, Love-Notes, Sincerity, Respect, etc.—some of them villages known to Cathos—to Love-on-Esteem, though one must take care not to go too far to the right, by way of Negligence, Lightness, and Forgetfulness, and fall into the Lake of Indifference; or, one may go to the left, avoiding the high Rock of Pride, and pass through Submissiveness, Slight-Attentions, Assiduity, Great-Services, Obedience, Constancy, etc., to Love-on-Gratitude.

In the villages of Wit, Familiar-Verse, Polite-Epistles, etc., the *précieuses* and *précieux* (ladies and gentlemen of culture) exercised themselves at all the minor literary *genres*—madrigals, rondeaux, sonnets, enigmas, impromptus—in which Mascarille boasts his prowess; and their writings were published in the " Choice Collection of Miscellanies " (*Recueil des pièces choisies*) to which Benserade, Scudéry, Boisrobert, and the great Corneille himself, among many others, contributed. In prose, the favourite exercises were letters and portraits: epistles which were meant rather for the printer than for the postman, and rather for the parlour than for the printer, and were read aloud to admiring groups; and portraits in which, impromptu (after much careful preparation), one of the company drew in words a character-sketch of another, or of himself. In one of Mlle. de Scudéry's novels a whole day (and half a volume), are devoted to this last exercise; no wonder that Madelon is " furiously fond " of it, and thinks " nothing so elegant."

In this affected society the French language, after being polished, was now being enervated ; the direct and simple word was avoided, and a spade was never called a spade. Even the names of the heroines were changed, for " just plain Kate " would never fit " in cultured style." The founder of the movement, the Marquise de Rambouillet herself, was known as " the incomparable Arthénice "—Arthénice being the romantic anagram of her plain name Catherine. Mlle. de Scudéry modestly called herself Sappho. Often the assumed names

were taken from novels, as were those of Madelon
(from *Le Roman de Polixène*) and Cathos (from Gomber-
ville's *Polexandre*); even their footman has a romantic
name, Almanzor, also taken from the *Polexandre*. The
précieuses greatly overworked some words, such as the
adverbs "furiously," "ferociously," "frightfully," and
"awfully"; and deprived the language of others, on
pretext of their being inelegant or coarse. They were
especially fond of circumlocution, which sometimes
went so far that their talk became unintelligible except
to the initiated. Some of the expressions which they
introduced became established in the language, such as
"dryness of conversation" (*sécheresse de conversation*),
but many of their locutions were too ridiculous to last,
and fully justified Molière's satire, since some of the most
extravagant which he brings into his play, such as "com-
modities of conversation" for chairs, and "counsellor of
graces" for mirror, were actually in use at the time.
Molière, the disciple of Rabelais and Montaigne, and
the lover of all that was direct, exact, and expressive in
language, could not well tolerate this sort of affectation.

He found the public ready and delighted to agree
with him. Many of the *précieux* were of the highest
rank and influence, and (probably through their efforts)
Molière was not allowed to give his play for two weeks
after the first performance. Then it was given forty-
eight times within a year, which was a remarkable success for that day, when the established stock company,
with its limited public, necessarily had a large and
constantly changing repertory. Most of the true *précieux* and *précieuses* were clever enough to see that it
was better policy for them to laugh at this caricature of
their ridiculous imitators, than to admit by their opposi-
tion that they were themselves open to such satire.
Molière, too, always clever and politic on his own

account, insisted in his preface to the play when it was published that "the true *précieuses* would be wrong to take offence when the ridiculous ones, who imitate them ill, are made fun of." But the shaft was shot. Ménage, one of the chief of the *précieux* wits, tells us in his *Memoirs* that the whole circle of the Hôtel de Rambouillet attended the first performance, and that he himself said to Chapelain at the end of the play : "Sir, you and I used to approve all the foolishness which has just been criticised so cleverly and with so much good sense ; but believe me, as St. Remy said to Clovis, we must burn what we used to worship, and worship what we used to burn." "And so it came to pass, continues Ménage in his *Memoirs*, "just as I had foretold; from the day of that first performance, fustian and artificial style were done with." It is very doubtful whether Ménage's story, published thirty-four years after that first performance, can be trusted ; especially since on no other occasion of his life did he show so much perspicacity. But the story is all the more significant for being probably untrue. And the effect of Molière's comedy is best shown by what one of its victims, some thirty years after, feels that it would have sounded well for him to say on that occasion. Of similar authenticity—and significance—are the stories of the old man who shouted from the pit: "Courage, Molière, that's good comedy!"—and of Molière's own comment on his success: "I no longer need to study Plautus and Terence, or patch together the fragments of Menander. I need only study the life about me."

CHARACTERS

		ACTORS
LA GRANGE DU CROISY } Rejected suitors.........		{ LA GRANGE DU CROISY
GORGIBUS, a worthy citizen...................L' ÉPY		
MADELON, daughter of Gorgibus CATHOS, niece of Gorgibus } would-be fine ladies.....		{ Mlle. DEBRIE ———————

MAROTTE, maid to the young ladies..MADELEINE BÉJART

ALMANZOR, footman to the young ladies..

The MARQUIS OF MASCARILLE, valet to
La Grange.............................. MOLIÈRE

The VISCOUNT JODELET, valet to Du Croisy. JODELET

Two chair-men

Neighbours

Musicians

THE AFFECTED MISSES

A COMEDY

SCENE I

LA GRANGE, DU CROISY

DU CROISY

Mr. La Grange.

LA GRANGE

What?

DU CROISY

Just look at me a moment, and don't laugh.

LA GRANGE

Well!

DU CROISY

What do you say to our call? Are you highly pleased with it?

LA GRANGE

Have we reason to be, do you think?

DU CROISY

Not entirely, to tell the truth.

LA GRANGE

For my part, I'll own I'm quite put out about it.

Tell me, did ever anybody see a pair of impudent country wenches put on such airs, or two men treated with more disdain than we were? They could hardly bring themselves to order chairs for us. I never saw such whispering as there was between them, such yawning, such rubbing of the eyes, and such constant asking: "What o'clock is 't?" Did they answer anything but "Yes." and "No" to all that we could say to them? And in short, will you not agree with me that, had we been the meanest creatures on earth, we could not have been worse used than we were?

DU CROISY

Methinks you take the matter much to heart.

LA GRANGE

Indeed I do, and so much so that I am determined to be revenged for their impertinence. I know what made them despise us. The affectation of culture has not only infected Paris, but it has spread through the provinces, and our ridiculous misses have inhaled their fair share of it. In a word, they are a dubious compound of the coquette and the would-be lady of culture. I see what a man must be if he wants them to receive him well; and if you 'll listen to me, we 'll combine to play them a trick which shall make them see their folly, and may teach them to know who 's who a little better.

DU CROISY

And how shall this be done?

LA GRANGE

I have a certain valet, called Mascarille, who in

the estimation of many people passes for a sort of a wit; for nothing is cheaper than wit nowadays. He is an odd piece, and has taken it into his head to ape the man of quality. He has a way of priding himself on gallantry and poetry, and disdains the other valets, even so far as to call them brute beasts.

DU CROISY

Well, what do you mean to do with him?

LA GRANGE

What I mean to do with him? We must . . . . But let's leave here first.

SCENE II

GORGIBUS, DU CROISY, LA GRANGE

GORGIBUS

Well! You 've seen my niece and my daughter? Will it be a success? What is the result of your call?

LA GRANGE

That is something you may better learn from them than from us. All we can say is, that we thank you for the favour you have done us, and remain your most humble servants.

DU CROISY

Your most humble servants.

GORGIBUS, *alone*

So–ho! They seem to be going away ill-satisfied. What can be the cause of their displeasure? I must find out about it. Ho there!

SCENE III

GORGIBUS, MAROTTE

MAROTTE

What do you wish, sir?

GORGIBUS

Where are your mistresses?

MAROTTE

In their chamber.

GORGIBUS

What are they doing?

MAROTTE

Making cold cream for their lips.

GORGIBUS

There's too much of this creamation; tell them to come down.

SCENE IV

GORGIBUS, *alone*

I think these hussies, with all their cream and stuff, have a mind to ruin me completely. I see nothing everywhere about but whites of eggs, nun's cream, and a thousand other tomfooleries that I know nothing about. They have wasted, since we've been here, the fat of a dozen sucking-pigs at least; and four servants might be fed every day on the sheeps' trotters they use.

SCENE V

MADELON, CATHOS, GORGIBUS

GORGIBUS

'Tis mighty needful to lay out so much on greasing your snouts! Just tell me what you did to those gentlemen, that I should find them going away so dissatisfied. Did n't I order you to receive them as the men I had picked out for your husbands?

MADELON

In what estimation, my dear father, would you have us hold the irregular procedure of those persons?

CATHOS

By what manner of means, my dear uncle, could a girl endowed with the least sense of things be reconciled to such individuals?

GORGIBUS

And what fault have you to find with them?

MADELON

A fine method of courtship is theirs! What! Begin immediately by proposing marriage?

GORGIBUS

And what would you have them begin by proposing? Concubinage? Is it not a manner of procedure that you both have reason to be gratified with, as well as I? Could anything be more complimentary, and is not their desire for this holy tie a proof of their honourable intentions?

MADELON

Oh! father, what you say is the depth of vulgarity.
It shames me to hear you speak in such fashion, and
you ought to take a few lessons in the elegant air of
things.

GORGIBUS

I have no use for the air nor for the song. I tell
you marriage is a holy and sacred thing, and 't is
acting honourably to begin by it.

MADELON

O Lud! If everyone were like you, how soon a
romance would be ended! A fine thing 't would be
if Cyrus married Mandane at once, and Aronce were
straightway wedded to Clélie!

GORGIBUS

What is the girl jabbering about?

MADELON

Father, here is my cousin who can tell you as well
as I that marriage must never come till after the
other adventures. A lover, to be agreeable, must
know how to utter fine sentiments, to breathe forth
the tender, the sweet, and the impassioned; and his
addresses must be made according to the rules.
First, he must see at church, or in the park, or at
some public ceremony, the one of whom he falls
enamoured; or else he must by fateful chance be
conducted to her house by some relative or friend,
and come away lost in musing and melancholy. For
a time he hides his passion from the beloved object,
and meanwhile pays her several visits, at which some
question of gallantry must without fail be brought

forward to exercise the wits of the company. Then comes the day of his declaration, which should oftenest be made in some garden-walk, while the rest of the company is at a little distance; and this declaration is followed by our sudden anger, shown in our blushes, which for a time banishes the lover from our presence. Next, he finds some means to appease us, to accustom us by insensible degrees to the recital of his passion, and to draw from us that avowal which costs us so much pain. After that come the adventures—rivals who cross and thwart an established affection, persecutions by fathers, jealousies arising from false appearances, complainings, despairs, abductions, and the rest. Thus are things conducted in high life; and these are rules which cannot be dispensed with in a genteel piece of gallantry. But to come point-blank to the conjugal union, to make love but when one makes the marriage contract, and to take the romance precisely by its tail!—I say again, father, nothing could be more like a common shop-keeper than such procedure; and my gorge rises at the mere imagination of it.[1]

GORGIBUS

What the devil of a gibberish is this I hear? There's the grand style for you with a vengeance.

CATHOS

Beyond a doubt, dear uncle, my cousin hits the truth of the matter. How can one receive people well who have no notion whatever of gallantry! I'll wager that they never saw the map of Love's-Land,[1]

[1] See the Introductory Note, p. 4.

and that Love-Notes, Slight-Attentions, Polite-Epistles, and Familiar-Verse are unknown countries to them. Can't you see that their whole presence shows it, and that they have not the air which gives you a good opinion of people at first sight? To come a-courting with a leg quite unadorned, a hat destitute of feathers, a head with undressed locks, and a coat that suffers an indigence of ribbons! Lud! What sort of lovers are those? What stinginess in dress, what barrenness of conversation! 'T is not to be endured, one can't abide it. I noticed likewise that their ruffs were not of the right make, and that their breeches lacked at least half a foot of being broad enough!

GORGIBUS

I think they are both gone mad, and I can understand nothing of their jargon. Cathos, and you, Madelon . . .

MADELON

Ah! pray, father, leave off those outlandish names, and call us otherwise.

GORGIBUS

How, those outlandish names? Are n't they the ones you were christened by?

MADELON

O Lud! how vulgar you are! For my part, 't is a thing that amazes me, that you could have got a daughter so clever as I. Did one ever hear, in cultured style, of Cathos or Madelon, and will you not own that one of them would be enough to disgrace the finest romance in the world?

CATHOS

'T is true, uncle, that an ear of the slightest delicacy is furiously excruciated when it hears those words pronounced; and the name of Polixena which my cousin has chosen, and that of Aminta which I have taken, possess a grace which you must needs acknowledge.[1]

GORGIBUS

Listen; one word shall settle the whole business. I won't let you have any names but those that were given you by your godfathers and your godmothers; and as for the gentlemen in question, I know their families and their fortunes, and I am determined you shall make up your minds to take them for husbands. I 'm tired of having you on my hands, and to keep a couple of girls is a bit too heavy a burden for a man of my age.

CATHOS

For my part, uncle, all I can say is that I consider marriage an altogether shocking thing. How can one endure the thought of lying by a man that 's really naked?

MADELON

Allow us a little breathing spell in the high society of Paris, where we have but just arrived. Let us weave at leisure the woof of our romance, and do not hasten its conclusion so much.

GORGIBUS, *aside*

No possible doubt of it, they are quite gone daft. (*Aloud.*) Once more, I understand nothing of all

---

[1] See the Introductory Note, p. 6.

this nonsense; but I am determined to be the absolute master; and, to put an end to all sorts of argument, either you shall both be married before very long, or, on my word, you shall both be nuns; I take my gospel oath on 't.

SCENE VI

Cathos, Madelon

CATHOS

O Lud! my dear love, how is the spiritual part of your father buried in the material! How thick are the windows of his intelligence, and how dark it is in his soul!

MADELON

What would you, my dear love? I am in confusion for him. I can hardly make myself believe that I am truly his daughter, and I think some adventure will yet discover for me a more illustrious birth.

CATHOS

I can well believe so; yes, there is every probability of it; and for my own part, when I look at myself, too . . .

SCENE VII

Cathos, Madelon, Marotte

MAROTTE

Here's a lackey asking whether you're at home; he says his master wants to see you.

MADELON

Learn, you dunce, to express yourself less vulgarly. Say: Here is a necessary evil that begs to know whether it is commodious for you to be visible.

MAROTTE

Gad! I don't know no Latin; and I've never learnt flossofy, like you did, out of the Grand Cyrus.

MADELON

The impertinent creature! How can one bear with it! But who is the master of this lackey?

MAROTTE

He said his name was the Marquis of Mascarille.

MADELON

Oh! my dear love, a marquis! Yes, go and say that we are visible. 'T is surely some wit who has heard us talked of.

CATHOS

Assuredly, my dear love.

MADELON

We must receive him in this lower room, rather than in our chamber. But at least let us arrange our hair a little, and try to do justice to our reputation. Quick, come within, and hold for us the counsellor of graces.

MAROTTE

Faith and troth, I don't know what sort of beast that be. You must talk Christian if you want me to understand you.

CATHOS

Bring us the mirror, you simpleton, and take good care not to sully its glass by the communication of your image.

SCENE VIII

MASCARILLE, TWO CHAIR-MEN

MASCARILLE [1]

Stop, porters! Hold! There, there, there, there, there! I think the rogues mean to break me in pieces by knocking me against the walls and pavements.

1ST CHAIR-MAN

Gad! 'T is because the door is narrow. Besides, you would have us come all the way in with you.

MASCARILLE

I should think so. You rascals, would you have

---

[1] In an account of the first performance of the play, by Mlle. Desjardins, herself a *précieuse* and a contributor to the *Choice Collection of Miscellanies*, there occurs this description of Mascarille's costume: "The Marquis entered so comically rigged out that I am sure I shall not displease you with a description of him. Imagine then a wig so long that it swept the floor each time he bowed, and a hat so small that you could plainly see he oftener carried it in his hand than on his head; his lace ruff was wide enough to make a respectable dressing-gown, and his stocking-rolls would have served admirably for children to play hide-and-seek in. A bunch of tassels hung from his pocket as if falling from a cornucopia, and his shoes were so covered with ribbons that 't is impossible for me to say whether they were of English calf or of morocco; all I know is that they were half a foot high, and I could hardly conceive how such tall and tiny heels could bear up the weight of this Marquis, with his ribbons, his rolls, and his powder."

me expose the rotundity of my feathers to the insults of the rainy season, and set the impress of my shoes upon the mud? Come, take your chair out of here.

2ND CHAIR-MAN

Then please to pay us, sir.

MASCARILLE

Eh?

2ND CHAIR-MAN

Please to give us our money, sir, I say.

MASCARILLE, *giving him a blow*

What, scoundrel, ask money of a person of my quality?

2ND CHAIR-MAN

Is that the way you pay poor folks? And will your quality help us to a dinner?

MASCARILLE

Ah! Ah! Ah! I 'll teach you to know your places! These dogs dare to make sport of me!

I^{ST} CHAIR-MAN, *taking up one of the poles of his chair*

Now then, pay us quick.

MASCARILLE

What?

I^{ST} CHAIR-MAN

I must have my money instantly, I say.

MASCARILLE

This fellow is reasonable.

1ˢᵗ CHAIR-MAN

Quick, I say!

MASCARILLE

Yes, yes! You speak properly, you do; but the other man is a rascal who does n't know what he is talking about. There, are you satisfied?

1ˢᵗ CHAIR-MAN

No, I 'm not satisfied; you gave my comrade a blow, and . . . (*raising his pole.*)

MASCARILLE

Gently; there, that is for the blow. People can get anything from me when they go the right way about it. Be off, and come back for me by-and-by to go to the Louvre, for the King's private Bed-chamber.

SCENE IX

MAROTTE, MASCARILLE

MAROTTE

The ladies will be down presently, sir.

MASCARILLE

Let them not hurry themselves; I am commodiously established here to wait for them.

SCENE X

MADELON, CATHOS, MASCARILLE, ALMANZOR

MASCARILLE, *after bowing*

Ladies, you 'll no doubt be surprised at the boldness of my visit; but your reputation brings this infliction upon you, and merit has such charms for me that I pursue it everywhere.

MADELON

If you are seeking merit, 't is not on our preserves that you should hunt.

CATHOS

To find merit with us, you must have brought it hither yourself.

MASCARILLE

Ah! I enter protest against your words. Fame tells but truth in boasting of your worth; and you will piquet, repiquet, and capot all that 's gallant in Paris.

MADELON

Your complaisance carries the liberality of its praises all too far; and my cousin and I will beware of accepting for earnest the sweets of your flattery.

CATHOS

My dear love, we should order more chairs.

MADELON

Ho there, Almanzor!

ALMANZOR

Madam.

MADELON

Quick, vehiculate hither the conveniences of conversation.

MASCARILLE

But, hold, is there any safety for me here?

(*Exit Almanzor.*)

CATHOS

What is 't you fear?

MASCARILLE

Some theft of my heart, some murder of my freedom. I see here eyes that look for all the world like dangerous fellows, ready to wrong one's liberties, and to treat a heart as Turks would use a Moor. What the devil! The moment you approach them, they are up in arms to slay. Ah! my faith, I mistrust 'em! And I'll e'en take to my heels, or else you'll give me bonds, and well endorsed, that they sha'n't hurt me.

MADELON

Dear love, he hath a pretty wit.

CATHOS

I see that he's a very Amilcar.[1]

MADELON

You have nothing to fear; our eyes have no evil designs, and your heart may sleep in confidence upon their honesty.

CATHOS

But, I beg you, sir, be not inexorable to that easy-chair that has been holding out its arms toward you this quarter of an hour; indulge a little its desire to embrace you.

[1] A character in Mlle. de Scudéry's *Clélie*, gallant and (supposedly) amusing.

MASCARILLE, *after having combed his wig, and arranged the lace rolls of his stockings*

Well! ladies, what say you to Paris?

MADELON

Alack! what could we say? One would have to be the antipodes of reason not to own that Paris is the great magazine of marvels, the centre of good taste and wit and gallantry.

MASCARILLE

For my part, I maintain that out of Paris there is no salvation for people of fashion.

CATHOS

That's an indisputable truth.

MASCARILLE

'T is a bit muddy here; but then one has the sedan.

MADELON

'T is true the sedan is a marvellous safeguard against the insults of mud and bad weather.

MASCARILLE

Do you receive abundance of visits? What great wit belongs to your set?

MADELON

Alas! we are not known yet; but we are in a way to be; and we have a special friend who has promised to bring here all the gentlemen who contribute to the *Choice Collection of Miscellanies*.[1]

---

[1] See Introductory Note, p. 5.

CATHOS

And certain others too, whom we have heard of as being the sovereign arbiters of elegancy.

MASCARILLE

'T is I who will manage this for you better than anybody; they all frequent me, and I may say that I never rise without half a dozen wits waiting upon me.

MADELON.

O Lud! we shall be obliged to you to the last degree if you will do us that kindness; for one must necessarily be acquainted with all those gentlemen if one would have a place in the polite world. 'T is they that make reputations in Paris; and you know there are some of them whose mere acquaintance is enough to give you the name of a connoisseur, even were there no other reason for it. But for my part, what I value most, is that by means of these intellectual visits one learns a hundred things which one needs must know, and which belong to the very essence of a real wit. One learns thereby, each day, the latest gossip of gallantry, and the pretty interchanges in prose and verse. One knows just on the moment: So-and-so has composed the finest piece in the world on such-and-such a subject; this lady has written words to that air; a certain gentleman has made a madrigal upon a favour received; another has composed stanzas on an infidelity suffered; Mr. So-and-so wrote yesterday evening a sixain to Miss Such-an-one, to which she sent her answer this morning about eight o'clock; such an author has made such-and-such a plan ; another is upon the third part of his romance ; another is putting his work through the press. This is what makes you to be thought much of in society, and if you know not these things, I would not give a pin for all the talent you may have.

CATHOS

In truth, I think 't is carrying the ridiculous to an extreme, when a person makes pretensions to wit, yet does not know even to the least little quatrain that is written every day ; and for my part, I should be in the depths of confusion should anyone ask me if I had seen something new that I had not seen.

MASCARILLE

'T is shameful, in good truth, not to have the first knowledge of everything that is written ; but do not be troubled about that ; I engage to establish an Academy of Wits in your house, and I promise you there shall not be a scrap of verse composed in Paris but you shall know it by heart before anyone else. For my part, even such as you see me, I make a pass at it when I 've a mind ; and you will find handed about, of my composition, in the cultured circles of Paris, two hundred songs, as many sonnets, four hundred epigrams, and more than a thousand madrigals, not to count riddles and portraits.

MADELON

I 'll own that I 'm furiously fond of portraits ; I think nothing is so elegant.

MASCARILLE

Portraits are difficult, and require a deep wit; you shall see some of my make that won't displease you.

CATHOS

As for me, I am terribly in love with riddles.

MASCARILLE

They exercise the wit, and I made four of them just this morning, which I 'll give you to guess.

MADELON

Madrigals are pleasant when they are neatly turned.

MASCARILLE

That is my own special talent; and I am now engaged on turning the whole of Roman history into madrigals.

MADELON

Ah! certes, that will be the very acme of beauty; I bespeak one copy at least, if you have it printed.

MASCARILLE

I promise each of you one, and in the best binding. 'T is beneath my rank; but I do it merely to give the booksellers, that pester me, a chance to make something.

MADELON

I fancy 't is a great pleasure to see oneself in print.

MASCARILLE

No doubt. But, by the way, I must recite for you an impromptu that I composed yesterday for a

duchess, a friend of mine, whom I was calling on;
for I am deucedly clever at impromptus.

CATHOS

The impromptu is the very touchstone of wit.

MASCARILLE

Then listen.

MADELON

We do, with all our ears.

MASCARILLE

Oh! oh! 't is not fair play, I say;
While you I view, sans thought of harm or grief,
Your eye doth slily snatch my heart away!
Stop thief! stop thief! stop thief! stop thief!

CATHOS

Oh! my Lud! that is carried to the utmost extreme of gallantry.

MASCARILLE

All I do has an off-hand, easy style; it does n't
smell of the pedant.

MADELON

'T is far from it—more than two thousand leagues
away.

MASCARILLE

Did you notice that beginning? *Oh! oh!* That
is something extraordinary, *oh! oh!* Like a man
that bethinks himself on a sudden, *oh! oh!* Taken
by surprise, *oh! oh!*

MADELON

Yes, I think that *oh ! oh !* admirable.

MASCARILLE

It seems a mere nothing.

CATHOS

O Lud! how can you say so? 'T is those sort of things that are beyond price.

MADELON

No doubt on 't, and I 'd rather have composed that *oh ! oh !* than an epic poem.

MASCARILLE

Egad! your taste is good.

MADELON

Eh! 't is not altogether bad.

MASCARILLE

But do you not admire also *'t is not fair play, I say?* *' T is not fair play, I say ;* you took me off my guard, I was not watching. A natural and familiar way of speaking, *'t is not fair play, I say.* *While you I view,* that is to say, I stand at gaze, I consider you, observe you, contemplate you. *Sans thought of harm or grief*, that is, innocently, without malice, like a poor silly sheep. *Your eye doth slily snatch . . .* What do you think of that expression *slily snatch?* Is it not well chosen?

CATHOS

Perfectly.

MASCARILLE

Slily snatch, as if from hiding; 't would seem as 't were a cat, in the very act of catching a mouse . . . *slily snatch.*

MADELON

Nothing could be better.

MASCARILLE

Doth slily snatch my heart away, carries it off, robs, abducts, steals it from me. *Stop thief! stop thief! stop thief! stop thief!* Would n't you think it was a man shouting and running after a thief to have him stopped? *Stop thief! stop thief! stop thief! stop thief!*

MADELON

It must be confessed that that has a most witty and gallant turn.

MASCARILLE

I 'll sing the air I 've composed for it.

CATHOS

Have you learnt music?

MASCARILLE

I? By no means.

CATHOS

Then how is this possible?

MASCARILLE

People of quality know everything without having ever learnt anything.

MADELON, *to Cathos*

Assuredly, my dear love.

MASCARILLE

See whether you find the air to your taste. *Ahem, ahem. La, la, la, la, la.* The brutality of the season has ferociously injured the delicacy of my voice. But no matter. 'T is in an easy, off-hand style.
(*Singing*)

Oh! oh! 't is not fair play . . . . etc.

CATHOS

Ah! that is indeed an impassioned air. Does it not kill you with delight?

MADELON

Yes, and there 's chromatics in it.

MASCARILLE

Don't you find the thought well expressed by the music? *Stop thief!* . . . And then, as if shouting at the top of one's voice, *stop, stop, stop, stop, stop, stop thief!* And then suddenly, like a person out of breath, *stop thief!*

MADELON

This it is to know the refinement of things, the grand refinement, the refinement of refinements. 'T is all marvellous, I assure you; I am enchanted with both air and words.

CATHOS

I never before saw anything so strong.

MASCARILLE

All that I do comes to me naturally, 't is unstudied.

MADELON

Nature has treated you as a fond mother indeed, and you are her spoiled child.

MASCARILLE

In what way do you pass your time, ladies?

CATHOS

No way at all.

MADELON

We have lived till now in a frightful fast from pleasures.

MASCARILLE

I am at your service to take you to the play one of these days, if you like; the more so as a new one is to be given, which I shall be very glad to have you see with me.

MADELON

'T is impossible to refuse.

MASCARILLE

But I beg you to applaud in proper fashion when we are there; for I have promised to cry up the play, and the author came to me again this morning to beg me to. 'T is the custom here that authors should come and read their new pieces to us people of quality, that they may win us to approve of them, and give them a reputation; and I leave you to im-

agine whether, when we say anything, the pit dare
contradict us! As for me, I am most scrupulous in
these matters; and when I have given my word to a
poet I always shout: Excellent! before the candles
are lighted.

MADELON

Oh! don't speak of it; Paris is an admirable place;
a hundred things happen here every day which you
cannot know in the provinces, however much a wit
you may be.

CATHOS

Enough; since we have been told, we will do our
duty, and cry out properly at every word that's
spoken.

MASCARILLE

I don't know whether I'm mistaken; but you
look for all the world as if you had written a play.

MADELON

Eh! there may be something in what you say.

MASCARILLE

Ah! my faith, we must see it. Between ourselves,
I have composed one that I mean to have acted.

CATHOS

Ah! . . . and to what players will you give it?

MASCARILLE

A pretty question! To the Royal Troup[1]; none

---

[1] That is, the actors of the Hôtel de Bourgogne, Molière's chief
rivals. They were more successful in tragedy than Molière, to his

but they can make things succeed; the others are ignorant fellows who speak their parts exactly as people talk; they don't know how to roll out a thunderous line, and pause at the fine passage; and how is one to know where the fine line is, if the player does n't stop at it and show us when to applaud?

CATHOS

Indeed, that is the way to make an audience feel the beauties of a work; and things succeed only so far as they are well set off.

MASCARILLE

How do you like my trimmings? Do you find them congruent to the coat?

CATHOS

Completely so.

MASCARILLE

The ribbon is well chosen.

MADELON

Furiously well. 'T is genuine Perdrigeon.

MASCARILLE

What do you say to my stocking-rolls?

MADELON

They are altogether stylish.

---

great chagrin, for it was his life-long ambition to succeed in serious plays, and he was constantly presenting tragedy as well as comedy at his theatre, especially during the first part of his career. But his acting was too realistic for the taste of his age, which could not take tragic actors seriously if they spoke their parts "exactly as people talk."

MASCARILLE

At least I may boast that they are a full quarter of a yard wider than any yet made.

MADELON

I must own I have never seen elegance of attire carried to such a height.

MASCARILLE

Just fasten the functions of your olfactory sense upon these gloves.

MADELON

They smell awfully good.

CATHOS

I never breathed a scent of higher quality.

MASCARILLE

And this one? (*He leans over and lets them smell the powdered hair of his wig.*)

MADELON

'T is unmistakably aristocratic; the upper region is deliciously titillated by it.

MASCARILLE

You've said nothing of my feathers; how do you find them?

CATHOS

Frightfully handsome.

MASCARILLE

Do you know, every tip cost me a gold louis. As

for me, 't is a passion with me always to go in for whatever 's most elegant.

MADELON

I assure you we are sympathetic natures, and I 'm furiously delicate in everything I wear; even to my under-socks, I cannot endure anything unless it be of the best make.

MASCARILLE, *crying out suddenly*

Oh! oh! oh! Gently. Damme, ladies, 't is very ill done; I have reason to complain of your behaviour, 't is not fair.

CATHOS

How now? What is the matter?

MASCARILLE

What! Both of you against my heart at once! Attacking me right and left! Ah! 't is against the law of nations; the match is not equal, and I shall cry out " Murder!"

CATHOS

One must confess that he says things in a way that is quite his own.

MADELON

He has an admirable turn of wit.

CATHOS

You are more frightened than hurt, and your heart cries out before its skin is scratched.

MASCARILLE

What the devil! It 's skinned from head to foot.

SCENE XI

CATHOS, MADELON, MASCARILLE, MAROTTE

MAROTTE

Madam, someone is asking for you.

MADELON

Who?

MAROTTE

The Viscount Jodelet.

MASCARILLE

The Viscount Jodelet?

MAROTTE

Yes, sir.

CATHOS

Do you know him?

MASCARILLE

He's my best friend.

MADELON

Show him in speedily.

MASCARILLE

'Tis a long time since we have seen other, and I am charmed at this chance meeting.

CATHOS

Here he is.

SCENE XII

CATHOS, MADELON, JODELET, MASCARILLE, MAROTTE, ALMANZOR

MASCARILLE

Ah! Viscount!

(*They embrace each other.*)

JODELET

Ah! Marquis!

MASCARILLE

How happy I am to meet with you!

JODELET

What joy is mine to find you here!

MASCARILLE

Just kiss me a bit more, I beg you.

MADELON, *to Cathos*

My dearest, we are beginning to be known; the polite world is finding its way to our door.

MASCARILLE

Ladies, allow me to introduce this gentleman; on my word, he is worthy of your acquaintance.

JODELET

'T is but justice to come and pay you your dues, and your charms assert their seigniorial rights over all sorts of persons.

MADELON

This is carrying your civilities to the utmost bounds of flattery.

CATHOS

This day should be marked in our calendar as a most happy day.

MADELON, *to Almanzor*

Come, boy, must we be always repeating things to you?   Don't you see we need the superaddition of an arm-chair?

MASCARILLE

Do not be astonished at seeing the Viscount look as he does.   He has but just recovered from an illness, which has made his face as pale as you see it.

JODELET

It is the fruit of late attendance at court, and of the fatigues of war.

MASCARILLE

Do you know, ladies, that you see in the Viscount one of the valiant men of his century?   He is a complete hero.

JODELET

You are no whit behind me, Marquis, and we know also what you can do.

MASCARILLE

It is true that we have seen each other in action.

JODELET

And in places where 't was very warm.

MASCARILLE, *looking at the two girls*

Yes, but not so warm as here.   Ha, ha, ha!

JODELET

Our acquaintance began in the army, and the first time we saw each other he was commanding a regiment of cavalry on board the galleys of Malta.

MASCARILLE

That is true; but still you were in service before I was, and I remember I was but a petty officer when you were in command of two thousand horse.

JODELET

War is a fine thing; but 'pon honour, nowadays men who have seen service, as we have, are mighty ill rewarded at court.

MASCARILLE

And that's why I mean to hang up my sword.

CATHOS

As for me, I have a furious weakness for military men.

MADELON

I adore them, too; but I would have wit to wait on courage.

MASCARILLE

Viscount, do you remember that half-moon we won from the enemy at the siege of Arras?

JODELET

What do you mean with your half-moon? Why, man, 't was a good full one, no less.

MASCARILLE

I believe you are right.

JODELET

I ought to remember it, 'pon honour! I got a wound there in the leg from a hand-grenade, that I bear the marks of still. Just feel it, I beg you; you 'll see what a wound it was.

CATHOS, *after having touched the place*

'T is true, the scar is large.

MASCARILLE

Give me your hand a moment, and feel this one, there, exactly at the back of the head. Do you find it ?

MADELON

Yes, I feel something.

MASCARILLE

That is a musket-wound I got in my last campaign.

JODELET, *baring his chest*

Here is another wound which pierced me quite through the body at the attack on Gravelines.

MASCARILLE

I will show you a furious cut.

MADELON

'T is not necessary; we believe it without seeing.

MASCARILLE

These are honourable scars which prove what one is.

CATHOS

We have no doubt of what you are.

MASCARILLE

Viscount, is your carriage here?

JODELET

Why?

MASCARILLE

We could take these ladies driving outside the gates, and offer them a little entertainment.

MADELON

We cannot go abroad to-day.

MASCARILLE

Then let us have musicians and dance.

JODELET

'Pon honour, 't is well thought on.

MADELON

As for that, we shall be pleased ; but there must be some increase of company.

MASCARILLE

Ho there ! Champagne, Picard, Bourguignon, Cascaret, Basque, La Verdure, Lorrain, Provençal, La Violette ! The devil take all lackeys. I think there 's not a gentleman in France worse served than I am. These scoundrels are always leaving me alone.

MADELON

Almanzor, tell the gentleman's servants to go seek for musicians, and fetch the gentlemen and ladies from hereabouts, to people the solitude of our ball.

(*Exit Almanzor.*)

MASCARILLE

Viscount, what do you say of those eyes?

JODELET

And you, Marquis, what think you of them?

MASCARILLE

For my part, I say that our freedom will have
much ado to get away clear and clean. At least I
am strangely pulled this way and that, and my heart
holds but by a single thread.

MADELON

How natural is all that he says! He gives a most
pleasing turn to everything.

CATHOS

'T is true, he makes a furious outlay of wit.

MASCARILLE

To show you my true quality, I will make an impromptu upon it. (*He meditates.*)

CATHOS

Oh! I beseech you with all the devotion of my
heart, let us have something that was composed for
us.

JODELET

I wish I might do as much; but I am a little ex-
hausted in my poetic vein, from the great number of
bleedings I have given it these past few days.

MASCARILLE

Oh, the deuce! I always get the first line well
enough; but I have trouble in making the others fit it.

Faith, this is a little too sudden ; I will make you an impromptu at my leisure, and you shall find it the finest in the world.

JODELET

He has the very devil of a wit.

MADELON

And gallant, and well turned.

MASCARILLE

Viscount, just tell me ; is it long since you have seen the Countess ?

JODELET

It's more than three weeks since I've called on her.

MASCARILLE

Do you know, the Duke came to see me this morning, and would have taken me down into the country to hunt a stag with him.

MADELON

Here come our friends.

SCENE XIII

Lucile, Celimene, Cathos, Madelon, Mascarille, Jodelet, Marotte, Almanzor, Musicians

MADELON

Lud, my dear loves, we ask your pardon. These gentlemen took a fancy to put heart into our heels ; and we sent for you to fill the voids of our assembly.

LUCILE

We are indeed obliged to you.

MASCARILLE

This is only a ball arranged in haste, but some day we will offer you one in due form. Are the musicians come?

ALMANZOR

Yes, sir; they are here.

CATHOS

Come then, my dear loves, take your places.

MASCARILLE, *dancing alone by way of prelude*

La, la, la, la, la, la, la, la.

MADELON

He has a perfectly elegant shape.

CATHOS

And looks to dance most properly.

MASCARILLE, *leading out Madelon to dance*

My freedom will dance the Courant as well as my feet. In time, fiddlers; in time. Oh! What boobies! 'T is impossible to dance with them. The devil take you! Can't you play in measure? La, la, la, la, la, la, la, la. Steady. O you country scrapers!

JODELET, *dancing also*

So, so! don't hurry the time so much; I have just recovered from an illness.

SCENE XIV

Du Croisy, La Grange, Cathos, Madelon, Lucile, Celimene, Jodelet, Mascarille, Marotte, Musicians

LA GRANGE, *stick in hand*

Ah! ah! you scoundrels! What are you doing here? We've been hunting for you these three hours.

MASCARILLE, *feeling the blows*

Oh! oh! oh! you did n't tell me there'd be blows in the bargain.

JODELET

Oh! oh! oh!

LA GRANGE

The idea of you, you scamp, trying to play the man of consequence!

DU CROISY

That 'll teach you to know your places.

SCENE XV

Cathos, Madelon, Lucile, Celimene, Mascarille, Jodelet, Marotte, Musicians

MADELON

What is the meaning of this?

JODELET

'T is on a wager.

CATHOS

What! Let yourselves be beaten in such fashion!

MASCARILLE

Gad! I did n't want to take any notice of it; for

I am of a violent temper, and I should have lost my self-control.

MADELON

Suffer such an affront in our presence!

MASCARILLE

'T is nothing; let us go on just the same. We have known them a long while; and between friends one should not take offence at such a trifle.

SCENE XVI

DU CROISY, LA GRANGE, MADELON, CATHOS, CELIMENE, LUCILE, MASCARILLE, JODELET, MAROTTE, Musicians

LA GRANGE

On my word, you rascals, you shall not make sport of us, I promise you. Come in, you there.

(*Enter three or four bullies.*)

MADELON

What means this impudence, to come and disturb us so in our own house?

DU CROISY

What, ladies! Shall we suffer our own lackeys to be better received than ourselves, and let them make love to you at our expense, and give you a ball?

MADELON

Your lackeys?

LA GRANGE

Yes, our lackeys; 't is neither handsome nor honourable to spoil good servants for us as you are doing.

MADELON

O heavens! what insolence!

LA GRANGE

But they shall not have the advantage of using our clothes to capture your fancy with; and if you are determined to love them, on my word, it shall be for their own fine looks. Quick, let them be stripped at once.

JODELET

Farewell our finery.

MASCARILLE

Thus are the Marquisate and Viscountship laid low.

DU CROISY

Ah! ah! you rascals, will you have the impudence to poach on our preserves? You must go and seek elsewhere the means of making yourselves agreeable in the eyes of your mistresses, I'll have you know.

LA GRANGE

'T is too much to supplant us, and that too with our own clothes.

MASCARILLE

O Fortune! how great is thy inconstancy!

DU CROISY

Quick, strip them down to the least thing.

LA GRANGE

Carry off all these duds, and be quick about it. Now, ladies, in the condition they are in, you may continue your amours with them as much as you please. As to that we leave you entire freedom, and we both protest to you that we shall not be jealous in the least.

SCENE XVII

MADELON, CATHOS, JODELET, MASCARILLE, Musicians

CATHOS

Oh! what humiliation!

MADELON

I am bursting with spite.

ONE OF THE MUSICIANS, *to the Marquis*

How is this now? Where do we come in, and who's going to pay us?

MASCARILLE

Ask the Viscount.

ONE OF THE MUSICIANS, *to Jodelet*

Who will give us our money?

JODELET

Ask the Marquis.

SCENE XVIII

GORGIBUS, MADELON, CATHOS, JODELET, MASCARILLE, Musicians

GORGIBUS

Ah, you jades, you've got us into a fine pickle, by what I can make out; and I've learned of great doings indeed from those gentlemen who have just gone.

MADELON

Oh! father, 't is a cruel trick they have played us.

GORGIBUS

Yes, it's a cruel trick, but you may thank your own foolish impudence for it, you sluts! They have paid back the usage you gave them, and I, worse luck, must swallow the insult.

MADELON

Ah! I swear we'll be revenged, or I shall perish in the attempt. And you, you rogues, dare you stay here after your insolence?

MASCARILLE

Treat a marquis in such fashion! That is the way of the world. The least misfortune changes love to scorning. Come, comrade, let's go seek our fortunes elsewhere. I see that here they care for naught but vain show, and hold in no esteem mere naked virtue.

(*Exeunt both.*)

SCENE XIX

GORGIBUS, MADELON, CATHOS, Musicians

ONE OF THE MUSICIANS

Sir, we expect you to pay us, since they have failed to, for our playing here.

GORGIBUS, *beating them*

Yes, yes, I'll pay you; and this is the coin I'll

pay you in. And you, you hussies, I don't know what keeps me from doing as much by you. We shall be the common talk and laughing-stock of everybody; and that is what you 've brought upon yourselves by your tomfooleries. Go hide yourselves, you worthless baggages; go hide yourselves forever. (*Alone.*) And you, that are the cause of their folly, silly trumpery, pernicious pastimes of empty minds, romances, verses, songs, sonnets, and sonnettas, the devil take you all!

LE

MEDECIN MALGRE LUI

COMEDIE EN TROIS ACTES

6 AOUT, 1666

———

THE DOCTOR BY COMPULSION

A COMEDY IN THREE ACTS

AUGUST 6, 1666

(*The original is in prose*)

INTRODUCTORY NOTE

"My public," said Molière (at least according to the legend), "could never be induced to accept sustained elevation in style and sentiments." As Professor Matthews has so well expressed it : "Molière felt it to be his duty always to keep his company supplied with plays of a kind already proved to be popular. So . . . he went back unhesitatingly to his earlier manner again and again, and no more thought it unworthy of himself to write frank farces like *The Doctor by Compulsion* after *Tartuffe* than Shakspere did to compose *The Merry Wives of Windsor* after *The Merchant of Venice*." It is also not impossible that Molière, as well as his public, took real delight and found real relief in this return to the frank farce, after the elevation of his more serious plays. In any case, the "step backward," as it has often been called by his critics, was at the same time a step forward, since in *The Doctor by Compulsion* he produced what is on the whole the best of his many farces ; and a really good farce is almost as rare as a good comedy of character. *The Doctor by Compulsion* occupies as high a place in its own literary class or *genre* as *The Misanthrope* in its class.

The story of the peasant who acts as a physician under compulsion of the cudgel, and performs marvellous cures, is as old as the Sanskrit collections of tales, and had been the subject of a mediæval French *fabliau* (with which Molière was probably unacquainted), and perhaps of earlier farces of the same period and kind as *Lawyer Patelin*. Molière's first knowledge of it may however have come from some Italian comedy. Soon after his return to Paris he had given a brief play called *The Faggot-Binder*, which is not preserved, and perhaps (like most of the Italian comedies) was never written out. The play as we now have it combines the "Gallic humour" of the mediæval French farce (though the extreme coarseness of expression which had seemed to be the inevitable vehicle of that humour is in this case almost entirely avoided by Molière), with the general movement and clever intrigue of the Italian impromptu comedy. Molière, like Shakspere, borrowed everywhere, but made what he borrowed completely his own. In *The Doctor by Compulsion* he has given this story its final form, and has created what is perhaps the most popular of all modern farces. When it first appeared, it had twenty-six successive representations, as against twenty-one for *The Misanthrope ;* since 1680 it has been given at the *Théâtre français* oftener than any other play except *Tartuffe*. It has been almost equally popular in many other languages than French, and has been translated into Russian, Danish, Swedish, Turkish, Magyar, Greek, and Armenian.

Joyous and extravagant as the farce is, it is also significant as another of Molière's many attacks upon humbug and quackery in whatever form he found it. In fact, when the amazing state of medical science in the seventeenth century is known, Molière's satire on it hardly seems exaggerated. The chief and almost the only methods of treatment in use were purging and bleeding. The Medical Faculty of Paris denied the circulation of the blood ; arguing that if it did circulate, any loss of blood in one part of the body would be immediately supplied from the other parts, and so bleeding would be useless ; but bleeding is not useless, therefore the blood does not circulate. Molière was not far wide of the mark in suggesting that the gown made the doctor, as is attested by part of the form of oath prescribed for professors of medicine on taking office : " I swear to teach in a long gown with big sleeves, with a doctor's cap on my head, and a bow of scarlet ribbon on my shoulder." In an earlier play Molière had directly attacked the four chief physicians of the court, of one of whom, Desfougerais, the famous Guy Patin wrote at the time : " I do not think there is on earth a more persistent or more perverse charlatan than this wretched chemist . . . who kills more people with his antimony than three honest men can save with the usual remedies.   I believe that if this fellow thought there were anywhere in the world a greater quack than himself, he would try to get him poisoned."   Molière was to return to the charge in his last play, in which he sums up his opinion of the doctors, who were letting him die at only fifty-one years old, as follows : " Most of them are great classicists, can talk fine Latin, can give Greek names to all diseases and define and classify them, but as for curing them, that is a thing they have no knowledge of."

CHARACTERS	ACTORS

SGANARELLE, husband of Martine..........MOLIERE
MARTINE, wife of Sganarelle........... Mlle. DEBRIE
SQUIRE ROBERT, neighbour of Sganarelle ..
VALERE, attendant of Géronte ....
LUCAS, husband of Jacqueline
        [and servant of Géronte].......
GERONTE, father of Lucinde..............DU CROISY
JACQUELINE, nurse at Géronte's, and wife of
  Lucas................................
LUCINDE, daughter of Géronte.........Mlle. MOLIERE
LEANDRE, in love with Lucinde...........LA GRANGE
THIBAUT, father of Perrin ⎫
PERRIN, son of Thibaut.. ⎬ Peasants
                ⎭

THE DOCTOR BY COMPULSION

A COMEDY

ACT I

SCENE I

SGANARELLE *and* MARTINE, *enter quarrelling*

SGANARELLE

No, I tell you, I'll do nothing of the sort, and 't is my place to do the talking and be the master.

MARTINE

And I tell you, you shall do as I please; just because I'm married to you I don't have to put up with your freaks!

SGANARELLE

Oh! what a monstrous plague 't is to have a wife! and how truly speaks Aristotle when he says that a woman is worse than a devil!

MARTINE

Just listen to the learned man, with his dolt of an Aristotle.

SGANARELLE

Learned man, yes, indeed I am! Find me a faggot-binder who can argue, like me, about anything whatever, who has served a famous doctor for six years, and in the days of his youth knew his Accidence by heart.

MARTINE

Plague on thee for an eternal ass !

SGANARELLE

Plague on thee for an impudent baggage!

MARTINE

Curst be the day and the hour when I went and said yes!

SGANARELLE

Curst be the hornèd goat of a notary who made me sign my own ruin !

MARTINE

Faith, it's you who have reason to complain of that business, is n't it!—when you ought to be on your knees every moment thanking heaven that you have me for a wife! Do you think you deserved to get such a wife as I am ?

SGANARELLE

Of course not—you did me too great honour, did n't you, and I had reason to be satisfied the night of our marriage, had n't I? 'Sdeath! don't make me speak on 't; I might say such things . . .

MARTINE

What? What might you say ?

SGANARELLE

Never mind, drop the subject. Only, we know

what we know, and you were mighty lucky to get
me.

MARTINE

What do you mean by mighty lucky to get you?
A man who is bringing me to the poor-house, a sot,
a scoundrel, who's eating up all I possess . . .

SGANARELLE

You lie; I drink a good part of it.

MARTINE

Who's selling, piece by piece, everything in the
house! . . .

SGANARELLE

That is economical—living within one's means.

MARTINE

Who has taken my very bed from under me!

SGANARELLE

You'll get up all the earlier.

MARTINE

Who won't leave a stick of furniture in the whole
place . . .

SGANARELLE

It'll be all the easier to move.

MARTINE

And who does nothing from morning to night but
gamble and guzzle! . . .

SGANARELLE

That's to keep up my spirits.

MARTINE

And while you 're doing that, what do you expect me to do with my family?

SGANARELLE

Do whatever you please.

MARTINE

I have four poor little children on my hands . . .

SGANARELLE

Put them down.

MARTINE

And they 're all the time asking for bread.

SGANARELLE

Give them a whipping; when I have had plenty to eat and drink, I want everybody in my house to have their fill.

MARTINE

And do you think, you drunkard, that things can go on so forever?

SGANARELLE

Dear wife, softly, I beg you.

MARTINE

Do you expect me to put up with your insults and debauches forever?

SGANARELLE

Do not let us get angry, dear wife.

MARTINE

Do you think I can't find a way to bring you back to your duty?

SGANARELLE

Dear wife, you know my heart is not over patient, and my arm is fairly strong.

MARTINE

I don't care a snap for your threats.

SGANARELLE

My dear little wife, my sweet love, your hide's itching again, I see, just as usual.

MARTINE

I'll show you I'm not a bit afraid of you.

SGANARELLE

My dear better half, you evidently want to get something from me.

MARTINE

Do you think I'm frightened by your talk?

SGANARELLE

Sweet object of my vows, I'll box your ears.

MARTINE

Drunkard, sot that you are!

SGANARELLE

I shall beat you.

MARTINE

You wine-sack!

SGANARELLE

I shall thrash you.

MARTINE

You wretch!

SGANARELLE

I 'll curry your hide.

MARTINE

Rascal! blackguard! traitor! coward! villain! scamp! scoundrel! cheat! rogue! thief! . . .

SGANARELLE

So! you must have it then? (*Sganarelle takes a cudgel, and lays it on.*)

MARTINE, *screaming*

Oh! oh! oh! oh!

SGANARELLE

This is the only way to calm you down.

SCENE II

SQUIRE ROBERT, SGANARELLE, MARTINE

ROBERT

Hold! hold! hold! Fie on you! What's this? For shame! Plague on the scoundrel, to beat his wife so!

MARTINE, *her arms akimbo, driving him about the stage as she speaks, and finishing off with a blow*

But **I** choose to have him beat me.

ROBERT

Oh! I am quite willing then.

MARTINE

Whose business are you poking into?

ROBERT

I am in the wrong.

MARTINE

Is it any affair of yours?

ROBERT

Of course not.

MARTINE

Just look at this impudent meddler, who wants to keep husbands from beating their wives!

ROBERT

I take it all back.

MARTINE

What have you to do with it anyway?

ROBERT

Nothing.

MARTINE

Had you any call to poke your nose in?

ROBERT

No.

MARTINE

Just mind your own business.

ROBERT

I 've not another word to say.

MARTINE

I like being beat.

ROBERT

All right then.

MARTINE

It is n't at your expense.

ROBERT

True.

MARTINE

And you 're a fool to come and thrust your oar in where you 're not wanted.

ROBERT, *going over to the husband, who likewise drives him about the stage as he speaks, beats him with the same stick, and puts him to flight*

Neighbour, I beg your pardon most humbly. Go on, beat your wife, give her a good thorough drubbing; I 'll be glad to help you.

SGANARELLE

But I don't choose to, d 'ye see?

ROBERT

Oh! that 's different.

SGANARELLE

I will beat her, if I will; and if I won't beat her, I won't.

ROBERT

Very good.

SGANARELLE

She is my wife, and not yours.

ROBERT

True enough.

SGANARELLE

I don't take any orders from you.

ROBERT

Quite right.

SGANARELLE

I have no use for your help.

ROBERT

So be it.

SGANARELLE

And you are an impudent meddler to poke yourself into other folks' business. Learn that Cicero says: " 'Twixt the tree and your finger you must not thrust the bark." (*After driving him off, he comes back to his wife, and says, squeezing her hand :*)

SCENE III

SGANARELLE, MARTINE

SGANARELLE

There! Now let's make up. Shake on it.

MARTINE

Yes, after beating me so!

SGANARELLE

That 's nothing. Shake.

MARTINE

I won't.

SGANARELLE

What?

MARTINE

No.

SGANARELLE

Dear little wife!

MARTINE

Never.

SGANARELLE

Come, I say.

MARTINE

Not a bit of it.

SGANARELLE

Come, come, come.

MARTINE

No; I will be angry.

SGANARELLE

Fie! for such a trifle! Come, come.

MARTINE

Let me alone.

SGANARELLE

Shake, I say.

MARTINE

You've abused me too much.

SGANARELLE

Oh! come now, I ask your forgiveness; let's have your hand.

MARTINE

I forgive you; (*aside*) but you shall pay for it.

SGANARELLE

You are foolish to make so much of it; these trifles are needed, every little while, between friends; and five or six whacks with a stick, when folk love each other, just rub up affection. Come, I'm off to the woods, and you shall have more than a hundred faggots to-day.

SCENE IV

MARTINE, *alone*

Yes, go; whatever face I put on, I sha'n't forget my resentment; and I'm all on fire to find some way to punish you for the beatings you've given me. I know well enough that a woman always has one means ready of getting revenge on her husband; but that is too delicate a punishment for my hang-dog; I want a vengeance that'll sting him more smartly; the other would not really make up for his outrage.

SCENE V

VALERE, LUCAS, MARTINE

LUCAS, *to Valère, without seeing Martine*

By jink! we uns 've got a devil of a job; and I dunno what we be going to get by it.

VALERE, *to Lucas, without seeing Martine*

What can you expect, good Mr. Nurse? We must obey our master; and besides, we both have something at stake, in the health of his daughter, our mistress; for no doubt her marriage, which has been delayed by this illness, would bring us in something. Horace, who is a generous gentleman, has a good chance of winning her hand; and though she has shown a kindness for one Léandre, you know very well that her father would never consent to have him for son-in-law.

MARTINE, *musing, aside*

Can't I find out some trick to get even?

LUCAS, *to Valère*

But what maggot has he got in 's brain now, since all the doctors with all their Latin hevn't done her no good?

VALERE, *to Lucas*

You may find sometimes, by much seeking, what you can't find at first; and often in humblest places . . .

MARTINE, *still thinking herself alone*

Yes, I must be revenged, no matter what it costs.

Those cudgel-thwacks rise in my gorge, I can't digest them ; and . . .

(*She says all this musing, so that, paying no attention to the two men, she runs against them as she turns round; and then says :*)

Oh! gentlemen, I ask your pardon. I did n't see you ; I was hunting round in my head for something I can't seem to find.

VALERE

Everyone has troubles of his own in this world, and we likewise are seeking for something we should much like to find.

MARTINE

Might it be something I could serve you in?

VALERE

Perhaps so ; we are seeking to meet with some man of skill, some physician of special parts, to give some sort of relief to our master's daughter, who is seized with an affliction that has all at once taken from her the use of her tongue. A number of doctors have already spent all their science upon her ; but people are sometimes to be found who possess wondrous secrets, particular remedies of their own, and who can do what the others could not ; and that is what we are seeking for.

MARTINE, *aside*

Oh! what a trick heaven has sent me to be revenged on that scoundrel of mine. (*Aloud*) You never could have hit it better, to find what you are after; for we have a man here, the most wonderful man in the world for desperate maladies.

VALERE

And, pray, where can we find him?

MARTINE

You will find him now just over there; he cuts wood for a pastime.

LUCAS

A doctor cut wood?

VALERE

He passes his time a-gathering of simples, you mean?

MARTINE

No! He is an odd kind of man who amuses himself that way, freakish, crotchety, whimsical, one you 'd never take for what he is. He goes about dressed in fantastical fashion, affects sometimes to appear ignorant, keeps his learning hid under a bushel, and avoids nothing so much as to use the marvellous talents which heaven has given him for medicine.

VALERE

'T is a curious thing that all your great men have ever some crotchet, some small grain of madness, mixed in with their learning.

MARTINE

This man's madness is greater than you would believe, for it sometimes goes so far that he 'll have to be beat before he 'll own up to his skill; and I warn you that you 'll never be able to manage him or make him admit he 's a doctor, if the whim is on him, until you take a stick, and bring him, by a good thorough drubbing, to own up in the end to what he 'll try to hide from you at first. That is the way we do when we need him.

VALERE

This is a strange madness.

MARTINE

So 't is; but afterward you 'll see that he does wonders.

VALERE

What is his name?

MARTINE

His name is Sganarelle. But 't is easy to recognise him; he is a man with a big black beard, and he wears a ruff, and a coat of yellow and green.

LUCAS

A green and yaller coat! 'T is the parrot-doctor, then?

VALERE

But is it quite sure that he is so skilled as you say?

MARTINE

Why! 't is a man that works miracles. Six months ago a woman was given up by all the other doctors; they had thought she was dead for six hours, no less, and they were getting ready to bury her, when this man I 'm telling you about was brought there

by force.　And he but just took a look at her, and
put a bit of a drop of something or other in her
mouth; and that very instant she got up off her bed,
and began right away to walk up and down the
room as if nothing had happened.

LUCAS

Oh!

VALERE

That must have been a drop of elixir of gold.

MARTINE

Very possibly 't was.　Then again, less than three
weeks ago, a twelve-year old boy fell clear down
from the top of the steeple, and broke his head and
his arms and his legs on the pavement.　No sooner
had they brought this man of ours than he rubbed
him all over his body with a certain ointment he
knows how to make; and the boy immediately got
up on his feet and ran off to play marbles.

LUCAS

Oh!

VALERE

That man must possess the panacea.

MARTINE

There's no doubt about it.

LUCAS

Jiminy! yon's the very man for us.　Let's go
quick and fetch him.

VALERE

We thank you for the kindness you have done us.

MARTINE

Be sure you remember the caution I gave you.

LUCAS

Zooks! trust us for that. If there needs but a beating, 't is a cooked goose.

VALERE, *to Lucas*

We are very lucky to have had this encounter; and I draw from it, mark you, the best of good omens.

SCENE VI

SGANARELLE, VALERE, LUCAS

SGANARELLE, *off the stage, singing*

Tol de rol . . .

VALERE

I hear somebody singing, and cutting wood.

SGANARELLE, *enters, singing and holding a bottle; he does not see Valère and Lucas*

Tol de rol . . . Faith, I 've worked enough for one spell. Let me breathe a bit. (*He takes a drink, and then says:*) That wood there 's as salt as the very devil. (*Singing*)

> *How sweet to hear,*
> *My bottle dear,*
> *How sweet to hear,*
> *Your gurgle clear!*

All men would curse my luck, I fear,
  If thou wert full forever.
Ah, bottle, bottle, doxy dear,
  Prithee be empty never.

Zounds! To it again! 'T were not right to breed melancholy.

VALERE, *aside to Lucas*

There's the very man.

LUCAS

I think that's a fact, and we's run right onto him.

VALERE

Let us look nearer.

SGANARELLE, *perceiving them, watches them carefully, turning from one to the other; he lowers his voice, and says, hugging his bottle:*

Ah, my little rascal! How I love thee, my little corksy-doxy! *All men . . . would curse . . . my luck . . . I fear . . . If . . .*
What the deuce! Who are these people after?

VALERE

'T is surely he.

LUCAS, *to Valère*

'T is him, the very spit an' image of him, just like what they told us.

SGANARELLE, *aside*

(*Here he sets his bottle on the ground, and as Valère bends over to bow to him, he, thinking Valère intends to take it away, sets it on the other side; then, as*

*Lucas does likewise, he takes it up again, and holds it
close, with many gestures, which make an amusing
pantomime.*)

They are watching me, and consulting. What can
they be after?

VALERE

Sir, is not your name Sganarelle?

SGANARELLE

Eh? What?

VALERE

I ask you if you are not the man named Sganarelle.

SGANARELLE, *turning toward Valère, then toward Lucas*

Yes, and no, according to what you want with
him.

VALERE

We only want to show him all the civilities that
we may.

SGANARELLE

In that case, 't is me that 's named Sganarelle.

VALERE

Sir, we are charmed to see you. We have been
sent to you for what we are in search of; and we
come to beseech your aid, which we greatly need.

SGANARELLE

If it is anything, gentlemen, which has to do with
my little trade, I am very ready to serve you.

VALERE

Sir, it is too much grace you do us. But, sir, be covered, pray; the sun might incommode you.

LUCAS

Clap it on, Master!

SGANARELLE, *aside*

These people are mighty full of ceremony. (*He puts on his hat.*)

VALERE

Sir, you must not be surprised at our coming to you. Men of skill are always sought after, and we have been informed of your ability.

SGANARELLE

'T is true, sirs, that I am the first man in the world for making of faggots.

VALERE

Oh, sir . . .

SGANARELLE

I spare no pains, and make them in such fashion there 's no fault to be found.

VALERE

Sir, that is not the point.

SGANARELLE

But then, I sell them at a hundred and ten sous per hundred.

VALERE

Do not say such things, I beg you.

SGANARELLE

I assure you I can't sell them for less.

VALERE

Sir, we know what is what.

SGANARELLE

If you know what 's what, then you know that 's my price.

VALERE

Sir, you are fooling with us to . . .

SGANARELLE

I 'm not fooling at all ; I can't come down one bit.

VALERE

Let us change our tone, I beg you.

SGANARELLE

You may get them cheaper somewhere else ; there are faggots and faggots ; but for those that I make . . .

VALERE

Oh, sir, let us talk no more of it.

SGANARELLE

I swear you shall not have them for a sou less.

VALERE

Oh ! fie !

SGANARELLE

No, on my conscience ; that is what you must pay. I mean just what I say, and I 'm not the man to overcharge you.

VALERE

My dear sir, how can a person like you waste his time in such cheap pretences, and lower himself so far as to speak thus! How can so learned a man, so famous a doctor as you are, choose to hide himself from the eyes of the world, and keep his great talents buried!

SGANARELLE, *aside*

The man's mad.

VALERE

Pray, sir, do not keep up this farce with us.

SGANARELLE

What?

LUCAS

All this gammon bean't no good; we knows what we knows.

SGANARELLE

How? What? What are you driving at? Who do you take me for?

VALERE

For what you are, for a great doctor.

SGANARELLE

Doctor yourself! I'm no doctor, and never was.

VALERE, *aside*

His madness is on him. (*Aloud*) Sir, pray do not deny things any longer; and let us not come, I beg you, to unpleasant extremes.

SGANARELLE

To what?

VALERE

To certain measures that we should be very sorry for.

SGANARELLE

Gad! Come to whatever you please! I'm not a doctor, and I don't know what you're driving at.

VALERE, *aside*

I see plainly that we must use the medicine. (*Aloud*) Sir, once more, I beg you to admit what you are.

LUCAS

Hey, deuce take it! don't shilly-shally no longer, speak up and own that you be a doctor.

SGANARELLE

This makes me furious.

VALERE

Why deny what every one knows?

LUCAS

Why for's all this flim-flam? What's the good of it to you?

SGANARELLE

Gentlemen, in one word as well as in two thousand, I tell you I am not a doctor.

VALERE

You are not a doctor?

SGANARELLE

No.

LUCAS

You bean't a doctor?

SGANARELLE

No, I tell you.

VALERE

Since you will have it so, we must make up our minds to it. (*They both take sticks, and beat him.*)

SGANARELLE

Oh! Oh! Oh! Gentlemen, I am anything you please.

VALERE

Why, sir, do you force us to this violence?

LUCAS

What's the good o' putting us at pains to beat you?

VALERE

I assure you I feel all possible regret for it.

LUCAS

I take my oath I'm sorry for it, sure I am.

SGANARELLE

What the deuce do you mean, gentlemen? Pray you, is it for a joke, or because you both are daft, that you will have it I'm a doctor?

VALERE

What! You don't yield yet? Do you persist in denying that you are a doctor?

SGANARELLE

Devil take me if I am!

LUCAS

Bean't it true that you 's a doctor?

SGANARELLE

No, plague choke me! (*They begin again to beat him.*) Oh! Oh! Hold, sirs, enough! since you will have it so, I am a doctor, I am a doctor; apothecary too, an 't please you. I 'll agree to everything rather than be beat to death.

VALERE

Ah! that is good, sir; I am charmed to find you will listen to reason.

LUCAS

It does my heart good when I sees you talk like that.

VALERE

I beg your forgiveness, from the bottom of my heart.

LUCAS

I asks your parding for the freedom.

SGANARELLE, *aside*

Lord, can I be the one that's mistaken, and can I have become a doctor without knowing it?

VALERE

Sir, you shall not regret discovering to us what you are; and you will certainly find yourself well satisfied for it.

SGANARELLE

But, gentlemen, tell me, may you not be mistaken yourselves? Is it beyond doubt that I am a doctor?

LUCAS

Yes, faith and troth!

SGANARELLE

Really?

VALERE

Beyond all doubt.

SGANARELLE

Devil take me if I knew it!

VALERE

Why, you are the most skilful physician in the world.

SGANARELLE

Oh! Oh!

LUCAS

A doctor that's cured all kinds of troubles.

SGANARELLE

O Lord!

VALERE

A woman had been thought dead for six hours; she was all ready for burial, when, with a drop of something or other, you brought her to life, and made her straightway walk about the room.

SGANARELLE

The plague I did!

LUCAS

A little lad of a dozen year old had a fall from the top of a steeple and got his head and his legs and his arms broke, and you, with some nointment or nother, made him get up on his feet 'fore anybody could say Jack Robinson, and run off to play marbles.

SGANARELLE

The deuce I did!

VALERE

In a word, sir, you shall have satisfaction with us, and you shall be paid whatever you please, if you will but let us take you where we want to.

SGANARELLE

I shall be paid whatever I please?

VALERE

Yes.

SGANARELLE

Oh! I am a doctor then, and no mistake. I had forgotten it; but now I remember. What is the affair? Where must I go?

VALERE

We will take you there. It is to see a girl who has lost her speech.

SGANARELLE

Faith, I have n't found it.

VALERE, *aside to Lucas*

He likes his little joke. (*To Sganarelle*) Come along, sir.

SGANARELLE

Without a doctor's gown?

VALERE

We will get one.

SGANARELLE, *giving his bottle to Valère*

You, hold this; that's where I keep my potions. (*Then, turning toward Lucas and spitting*) You, step on that, by the doctor's orders.

LUCAS

By jink! here's a doctor as I likes. He 's safe to get on, for he 's a jolly dog.

ACT II

SCENE I

GERONTE, VALERE, LUCAS, JACQUELINE

VALERE

Yes, sir, I think you will be satisfied; we have brought you the greatest doctor in the world.

LUCAS

Oh! zooks! Need n't hunt no more, now you 've found *him!* All the others bean't fit to untie his shoes for him.

VALERE

'T is a man who has worked marvellous cures.

LUCAS

Who 's mended folks that was dead.

VALERE

He is a bit capricious, as I told you; and there are times when his wits go wool-gathering and do not show for what they are.

LUCAS

Ay, he likes to play clown; and sometimes a body might say, no offence to you, that he 's got a screw loose in his head.

VALERE

But, at bottom, he is all science; and he often says things quite sublime.

LUCAS

When he puts his mind to 't, he talks right off as if he was reading out of a book.

VALERE

His reputation has already spread abroad in these parts; and everyone waits upon him.

GERONTE

I have a vast desire to see him; send him to me at once.

VALERE

I will go fetch him.

SCENE II

Geronte, Jacqueline, Lucas

JACQUELINE

Faith an' troth, sir, this un 'll do just as good as the rest. I do think 't will be six one and half dozen t' other; and I say the best medicine anybody could give your darter would be a fine handsome husband that she had a fondness for.

GERONTE

Lord bless me, sweet nurse, you are over meddlesome!

LUCAS

Hold your tongue, huzzif Jacqueline; it bean't for you to stick in your oar.

JACQUELINE

I tell ye, and both o' ye, that all these doctors 'll do no more good than clear water; an' your darter wants summat else than rhubarb an' senna; and a husband's a plaster that cures all girls' ailments.

GERONTE

Would anyone burden himself with her now, with the affliction she has? And when I intended to marry her, did she not oppose my will?

JACQUELINE

I should think so; you wouldn't let her have none but a man she don't like. Why didn't you try Mister Liander, who'd gotten her heart?—Then she'd a been mighty obedient; and I'll warrant now that he'd take her, thar, just as she be, if you'd let him have her.

GERONTE

This Léandre is not the right man for her; he's not rich like the other one.

JACQUELINE

He's got an uncle who's ever so rich, an' he'll be his heredity.

GERONTE

All these riches in prospect seem to me worth no more than an old song. There's nothing so good as a bird in the hand; and you run a great risk of being well fooled, if you count on walking in dead men's shoes. Death doesn't always have his ears open to the vows and prayers of gentlemen heirs ; and your teeth 'll have time to grow long, if you wait for your living till someone else dies.

JACQUELINE

Well, anyhow, I've always hearn tell that in marriage, like in everything else, contentment is better than riches. Fathers and mothers have this cursed custom of always asking how much hev he got, an' how much hev she got. There's old neighbour Peter that went an' married his girl Simonette to fat Tammas, 'cause he had a bit of a vineyard more than young Robin that she'd set her heart on ; and now look at the poor thing, gone as yellow as a quince, and hev'n't got no good of anything ever since. There's a fine warning for you, Master. Nothing's any good in this world unless you're happy ; and I'd rather give my darter a lusty husband that she liked, than all the riches of India.

GERONTE

Plague on it, good Mrs. Nurse, how you do run on! Hold your peace, I pray you; you take too much upon yourself; and you'll overheat your milk.

LUCAS

(*While speaking to Jacqueline, he keeps strikiug Géronte on the chest.*)

Gazooks! Hold your tongue! you're an impudent hussy. Master has no need for your preachments, he knows his own business. You mind yours, and go nurse your baby, 'thout argyfyin' so much.

Master's the father of his own darter, and he's a
kind man and a wise one, and knows what's good
for her.

GERONTE

Oh! Gently! Hold! Stop!

LUCAS, *still striking Géronte*

Master, I'll mortify her a bit, and learn her the
respect she owes you.

GERONTE

Yes, but you need not gesticulate so.

SCENE III

VALERE, SGANARELLE, GERONTE, LUCAS, JACQUELINE

VALERE

Sir, prepare yourself.   Here comes our doctor.

GERONTE, *to Sganarelle*

Sir, I am charmed to receive you, for we are in
great need of you.

SGANARELLE, *in doctor's gown, and with a high-
crowned and very pointed hat*

Hippocrates says . . . let us both put on our hats.

GERONTE

Hippocrates says that?

SGANARELLE

Yes.

GERONTE

In what chapter, if you please?

SGANARELLE

In his chapter—on hats.

GERONTE

Since Hippocrates says so, it must be done.

SGANARELLE

Doctor, since I have learned of the marvellous cures . . .

GERONTE

To whom are you speaking, pray?

SGANARELLE

To you.

GERONTE

I am no doctor.

SGANARELLE

You are not a doctor?

GERONTE

No, indeed.

SGANARELLE

Do you mean it?

GERONTE

I do mean it. (*Sganarelle takes a cudgel and beats Géronte just as he had been beaten himself.*) Oh! Oh! Oh!

SGANARELLE

You are a doctor now ; I never had any other degree.

GERONTE, *to Valère*

What ruffian of a fellow have you brought me here?

VALERE

Remember, I told you he was a droll sort of doctor.

GERONTE

Yes, but I will send him packing with his drolleries.

LUCAS

Don't mind a little thing like that, Master; it 's only his bit of a joke.

GERONTE

This style of joking does n't suit me.

SGANARELLE

Sir, I beg your pardon for the liberty I have taken.

GERONTE

Sir, I am your humble servant.

SGANARELLE

I am exceedingly sorry . . .

GERONTE

Oh, it 's nothing at all.

SGANARELLE

For the cudgelling . . .

GERONTE

There is no harm done.

SGANARELLE

Which I have had the honour to give you.

GERONTE

Let us say no more of it.   Sir, I have a daughter who is fallen into a strange sickness.

SGANARELLE

I am overjoyed, sir, that your daughter has need of me; and I could wish with all my heart that you needed me too, you yourself and all your family, that I might prove to you my eager desire to serve you.

GERONTE

I am obliged to you for your good wishes.

SGANARELLE

I assure you that I speak from the bottom of my heart.

GERONTE

You do me too much honour.

SGANARELLE

What is your daughter's name?

GERONTE

Lucinde.

SGANARELLE

Lucinde!   Oh! a fine name to practise on!   Lucinde!

GERONTE

I 'll just go and see what she is about.

SGANARELLE

Who is that fine big woman?

GERONTE

She 's the nurse to a young child of mine.

SCENE IV

Sganarelle, Jacqueline, Lucas

SGANARELLE, *aside*

The deuce! That is a handsome piece of furniture! (*Aloud*) Oh! nurse, charming nurse, my doctory is the most humble slave of your nursery, and I would I were the lucky little bantling to suck the milk (*he puts his hand on her breast*) of your good graces. All my medicine, all my knowledge, all my skill, is at your service; and . . .

LUCAS

By your good leave, Master Doctor, let my wife alone, I say.

SGANARELLE

What! Is she your wife?

LUCAS

Yes.

SGANARELLE

Oh ! Really, I did not know that, and I am overjoyed for love of both of you. (*He makes as if he would embrace Lucas, and, turning round to the nurse, embraces her instead.*)

LUCAS, *pulling Sganarelle away*

Stop that, I say.

SGANARELLE

I assure you I am delighted to see you joined to-gether; I congratulate her on having a husband such as you are; (*Again he makes as if to embrace Lucas, and, slipping under his arms, throws himself upon the nurse's neck*) and I congratulate you, dear sir, on having a wife so handsome, so honest, and so buxom as she is.

LUCAS, *pulling him away again*

Hey! zooks! don't be so free with your compliments, d' ye hear?

SGANARELLE

Would you not have me rejoice with you in such a well-matched union?

LUCAS

With me as much as you like; but with my wife, not so much ceremonies.

SGANARELLE

I take an equal interest in both your good fortunes; (*The same by-play is repeated*) and if I embrace you to show you my joy therein, I embrace her to show likewise the same joy to her.

LUCAS, *pulling him away for the third time*
Oh! 'S bodikins, Mr. Doctor, what a deal o' non-sense !

SCENE V

GERONTE, SGANARELLE, LUCAS, JACQUELINE

GERONTE
Sir, my daughter will be here presently.

SGANARELLE
I await her, sir, with all my medicine.

GERONTE
Where is it?

SGANARELLE, *touching his forehead*
Within here.

GERONTE
'T is very well.

SGANARELLE, *trying to touch the nurse's breasts*
But, since I take such an interest in all your family, I must just try your nurse's milk a bit, and inspect her bosom.

LUCAS, *pulling him away, and whirling him round*
Nay, nay ; I 'll not stand that.

SGANARELLE
'T is the doctor's duty to see the nurse's nipples.

LUCAS
Don't duty me no duties, say I, by your leave, sir.

SGANARELLE

Are you so bold as to oppose the doctor's orders?
Out o' the way with you!

LUCAS

I don't care a snap for no doctor!

SGANARELLE, *eyeing him askance*

I 'll give you the fever.

JACQUELINE, *taking Lucas by the arm, and whirling
him round likewise*

Now you get out too; bean't I big enough to de-
fend my own self, if he does anything to me he hed n't
ought to?

LUCAS

I won't have him a-handling of you, I won't.

SGANARELLE

Fie on the lout, he 's jealous of his wife!

GERONTE

Here comes my daughter.

SCENE VI

LUCINDE, GERONTE, SGANARELLE, VALERE, LUCAS,
JACQUELINE

SGANARELLE

Is this the patient?

GERONTE

Yes.   She is my only daughter; and I should be
mortally sorry if she were to die.

SGANARELLE

Let her see to it she does n't! She must not die without the doctor's prescription.

GERONTE

Bring a chair, here.

SGANARELLE, *seated between Géronte and Lucinde*

'T is a patient that 's not so repulsive; I maintain that a man in full health might make shift to get on with her.

GERONTE

You have made her laugh, sir.

SGANARELLE

So much the better; when the doctor makes the patient laugh, 't is the best symptom in the world. (*To Lucinde*) Well! what 's the matter? What ails you? Where 's the pain?

LUCINDE *answers by signs, putting her hand to her lips and her head, and under her chin*

Haw, he, ho, haw.

SGANARELLE

Eh? What do you say?

LUCINDE *continues the same gestures*

Haw, he, ho, haw, haw, he, ho.

SGANARELLE

What?

LUCINDE

Haw, he, ho.

SGANARELLE, *imitating her*

Haw, he, ho, haw, ha.   I don't understand you.
What deuced language is this?

GERONTE

Sir, that is just her ailment.   She has gone dumb,
and as yet no one has been able to find out the
reason of it; and this unfortunate incident has
caused her marriage to be put off.

SGANARELLE

But why?

GERONTE

The man who is to marry her prefers to wait till
she is cured before he binds himself.

SGANARELLE

And who's this blockhead, that doesn't want his
wife to be dumb?   Would to God that mine had
that ailment!   I'd take good care not to have her
cured.

GERONTE

In a word, sir, we beg you to employ your utmost
skill to relieve her affliction.

SGANARELLE

Oh! don't give yourself any concern about that.
Just tell me: does this malady oppress her very
much?

GERONTE

Yes, sir.

SGANARELLE

All the better.   Does she feel any great pain?

GERONTE

Very great.

SGANARELLE

That is excellent.   Does she go —— you know where?

GERONTE

Yes.

SGANERELLE

Freely?

GERONTE

I understand nothing of that.

SGANARELLE

Is the matter laudable?

GERONTE

I am no expert in these things.

SGANARELLE, *turning toward the patient*

Give me your arm.   (*To Géronte*) Here's a pulse which shows—that your daughter is dumb.

GERONTE

Why! Yes sir, that is her ailment; you have found it out at once.

SGANARELLE

Ha! ha!

JACQUELINE

Just see how he guessed what ailed her!

8896

SGANARELLE

We great doctors know things instantly. An ig-
noramus would have been puzzled, and would have
beat about the bush, and said: "'T is this, 't is that";
not so I—I hit the mark at the first shot, and I
inform you—that your daughter is dumb.

GERONTE

Yes; but I would you could tell me whence it
comes.

SGANARELLE

There is nothing easier; it comes from her having
lost her speech.

GERONTE

Very good. But what is the cause, I pray you,
that has made her to lose her speech?

SGANARELLE

All our best authors will tell you that 't is an impediment in the action of her tongue.

GERONTE

But once more, what are your ideas upon this impediment in the action of her tongue?

SGANARELLE

Aristotle, on that head, says . . . mighty fine
things.

GERONTE

I believe you.

SGANARELLE

Ah! he was a great man!

GERONTE

There is no doubt of it.

SGANARELLE

Altogether a great man ; (*Holding out his arm from the elbow*) a man who was greater than I am by fully that much. But, to come back to our argument, I hold that this impediment in the action of her tongue is caused by certain humours which we men of science call peccant humours ; peccant, that is to say . . . peccant humours ; inasmuch as the vapours formed by the exhalations of the influences that arise in the region of distempers, coming . . . so to speak . . . to . . . Do you understand Latin?

GERONTE

Not in the least.

SGANARELLE, *starting up*

You don't understand Latin?

GERONTE

No.

SGANARELLE, *taking various comic poses*

Cabricias arci thuram, catalamus, singulariter, nominativo, haec Musa "the Muse," *bonus, bona, bonum, Deus sanctus, estne oratio latinas? Etiam,* "Yes." *Quare?* "Why?" *Quia substantivo et adjectivum concordat in generi, numerum, et casus.*

GERONTE

Ah! why did I not study?

JACQUELINE

What a clever man is that!

LUCAS

Yes, it 's so fine I don't understand no jot of it.

SGANARELLE

Now, these vapours I tell you of, passing from the left side, where the liver is, to the right side, where the heart is, it happens that the lung, which we call in Latin *armyan*, having connection with the brain, which we name in Greek *nasmus*, by means of the hollow vein, which we denominate in the Hebrew *cubile*, meets on its way the said vapours which fill the ventricles of the omoplate ; and because the said vapours . . . follow my reasoning closely, I beg you ; and because the said vapours have a certain malignity . . . listen carefully to this, I adjure you.

GERONTE

Yes.

SGANARELLE

Have a certain malignity which is caused . . . pay attention, if you please.

GERONTE

I am doing so.

SGANARELLE

Which is caused by the acridity of the humours engendered in the concavity of the diaphragm, it comes to pass that these vapours . . . *Ossabandus, nequeis, nequer, potarinum, quipsa milus.* And that is exactly why your daughter is dumb.

JACQUELINE

Oh ! how fine that was spoke, my man !

LUCAS

If I had but as free a tongue as him!

GERONTE

'T is impossible to reason better, I am sure. Only one thing gave me pause: 't is the whereabouts of the liver and the heart. Methinks you placed them otherwise than as they are; and that the heart is on the left side, and the liver on the right.

SGANARELLE

Yes, that used to be so; but we have changed all that; and now we practise medicine in an entirely new fashion.

GERONTE

Ah!—I did not know that, I beg your pardon for my ignorance.

SGANARELLE

There is no harm done; you are not under obligation to be as learned as we are.

GERONTE

Certainly not. But, sir, what think you we must do for this malady!

SGANARELLE

What I think we must do?

GERONTE

Yes.

SGANARELLE

My opinion is that she should be put back in bed,

and made to take as medicine plenty of bread dipt in wine.

GERONTE

Why that, sir?

SGANARELLE

Because there is in wine and bread, taken together, a sympathetic virtue that loosens the tongue. Do you not know that they give nothing but this to parrots, who learn to talk by eating it?

GERONTE

That is true! Oh! what a great man! Quick, plenty of bread and wine.

SGANARELLE

I will come back toward evening to see how she is.

SCENE VII

GERONTE, SGANARELLE, JACQUELINE

SGANARELLE, *to Jacqueline*

You, stay a bit. (*To Géronte*) Sir, here is a nurse to whom I must apply some little remedies.

JACQUELINE

Who? me? I'm as sound as a roach.

SGANARELLE

So much the worse, nurse; so much the worse. This high health is a dangerous thing, and 't will not be amiss to give you a little gentle bleeding and to administer to you some slight mollifying injection.

GERONTE

But, sir, that is a method which I do not understand.   Why be bled when one is not ill?

SGANARELLE

No matter.   The method is a salutary one; and,
just as we drink for the thirst to come, so must we
be bled for the illness to come.

JACQUELINE, *going*

Faith, I care naught for that, and I won't go and
make a 'pothecary shop o' my carcase.

SGANARELLE

You rebel against medicine; but we shall find a
way to bring you to reason.

SCENE VIII

Geronte, Sganarelle

SGANARELLE

I give you good day.

GERONTE

Wait a little, please.

SGANARELLE

What do you want?

GERONTE

To give you your fee, sir.

SGANARELLE, *holding out his hand behind him from under his gown, while Géronte is opening his purse*

I shall take none, sir.

GERONTE

Sir . . .

SGANARELLE

By no means.

GERONTE

Just a moment.

SGANARELLE

Not for anything.

GERONTE

I pray you !

SGANARELLE

What an idea !

GERONTE

There you have it.

SGANARELLE

I shall not take it.

GERONTE

Oh !

SGANARELLE

'T is not for money I practise.

GERONTE

I believe you.

SGANARELLE, *having taken the money*

Is this full weight?

GERONTE

Yes, sir.

SGANARELLE

I am not a mercenary doctor.

GERONTE

I am sure of that.

SGANARELLE

I am not governed by self-interest.

GERONTE

Far be it from me to think so.

SGANARELLE, *alone, looking at the money he has received*

Faith, this is not so bad; and if only . . .

SCENE IX

LEANDRE, SGANARELLE

LEANDRE, *to Sganarelle*

Sir, I have been waiting for you a long while; I have come to beseech your assistance.

SGANARELLE, *taking his wrist*

This is a very bad pulse.

LEANDRE

I am not ill, sir; that is not what I have come to you for.

SGANARELLE

If you are not ill, why the deuce don't you say so?

LEANDRE

No.   To tell you in a word how things stand, my

name is Léandre, and I am in love with Lucinde, to whom you have just paid a visit; and since, through the ill-will of her father, it is impossible for me to come near her, I venture to beg that you will be so good as to serve my love, and give me the chance to carry out a stratagem I have invented in order to say to her a few words on which my happiness and my life absolutely depend.

SGANARELLE, *pretending to be angry*

For whom do you take me? How dare you come to me to serve you in your love-affair, and try to debase the dignity of a doctor to such low uses?

LEANDRE

Sir, don't make a disturbance.

SGANARELLE, *driving him back*

I will make a disturbance. You are an insolent puppy.

LEANDRE

Oh! sir, softly.

SGANARELLE

An ill-advised fool.

LEANDRE

I beg you!

SGANARELLE

I will teach you that I am not that kind of a man, and that it is a piece of extreme insolence . . .

LEANDRE, *taking out a purse and giving it to him*

Sir . . .

SGANARELLE

To wish to use me . . . (*Taking the purse*) I am
not speaking of you, for you are a gentleman, and I
should be charmed to serve you; but there are certain impertinent fellows in the world who go and
take people for what they are not; and I tell you
frankly that this puts me in a passion.

LEANDRE

I beg your pardon, sir, for the liberty I . . .

SGANARELLE

Do not speak of it.   What is it you want?

LEANDRE

You must know, sir, that this illness you are trying to cure is a sham.   The doctors have reasoned
upon it in fine style, and have not failed to say that
it came, one from the brain, one from the bowels,
one from the spleen, one from the liver; but 't is
certain that love is the true cause of it, and that
Lucinde has invented it only to deliver herself from
a marriage which was being forced upon her.   But,
for fear we should be seen together, let us withdraw
from here, and I will tell you on the way what I
desire of you.

SGANARELLE

Very well, sir; you have inspired me with an in-
conceivable sensibility for your love; and if I have
to spend all my science upon it, the patient shall
either give up the ghost or be yours.

ACT III

SCENE I

LEANDRE, SGANARELLE

LEANDRE

Methinks I do not make such a bad apothecary; and, as the father has scarce ever seen me, this change of dress and wig is enough, I imagine, to disguise me from him.

SGANARELLE

No doubt of it.

LEANDRE

All I could wish would be to know five or six long medical terms, to adorn my discourse and give me the air of a learned man.

SGANARELLE

Nonsense, all that is unnecessary; the gown is enough; I know no more of it than you do.

LEANDRE

What!

SGANARELLE

The devil take me if I know a thing about medicine. You are a gentleman, and I will trust you with my secret as you have trusted me with yours.

LEANDRE

What, you are really not . . .

SGANARELLE

No, I tell you; they made me a doctor maugre my teeth, as the old saying goes. I had never thought of being so learned as that; and all my studies had n't gone beyond the sixth class. I don't know what put this notion into their heads, but when I saw they were set on having me be a doctor, I made up my mind to be one, at the expense of whom it may concern. But you would never imagine how the error has spread, and how everybody is possessed to believe me a man of skill. They come for me from all parts; and, if things keep on so, I intend to stick to medicine all my life. I find it the best of all trades, for, whether we do well or ill, we are always paid just the same. We are not held to account for the bad work; and we cut away as we choose in the stuff we work on. A cobbler, making shoes, cannot spoil a scrap of leather without having to pay for the damage; but in our business we can spoil a man without its costing us a penny. The blunders are not put down to us, and the fault is always in him that dies. In short, the good thing about this profession is, that amongst the dead there exists an honour, a discretion, that cannot be surpassed; not one has ever been known to complain of the doctor that despatched him.

LEANDRE

'T is true that the dead are very well-behaved in this respect.

SGANARELLE, *seeing some men coming to him*

Here are some people who look as if they were coming to consult me. (*To Léandre*) Go and wait for me near your lady's house.

SCENE II

THIBAUT, PERRIN, SGANARELLE

THIBAUT

Master, we be come to look for you, son Perrin and me.

SGANARELLE

What is it?

THIBAUT

His poor mother, which her name be Parrette, has been laying sick abed these six months.

SGANARELLE, *holding out his hand as if to receive money*

What would you have me do about it?

THIBAUT

We'd hev you, Master, to give us some bit of druggery for to cure her.

SGANARELLE

I must see what 't is she's sick of.

THIBAUT

She's bad with hypocrisy, Master.

SGANARELLE

With hypocrisy?

THIBAUT

Yes, I mean she be swelled up all over; they say as how 't is from a lot of seriosities she hev got in her inside, and how that her liver, or her belly, or her spleen, whichever you likes to call it, 'stead of makin' blood, don't make nothin' but water. One day out o' two she 've the quotiguian fever, with lassitules and pains in the muzzles of her legs. You 'll hear flumes in her throat that seem like to choke her; and sometimes she 's took with singcups and conversions, so 't we think she 's gone off. We 've got in our village a 'potecary, savin' y'r presence, that 's give her no knowin' how much of his stuff; and it 've cost me more 'n a dozen good crowns in drenches, askin' your pardon, and in apostumes 't he makes her take, in hyacinth infections and in cordal portions. And all that, as t' other man said, wa' n't nowt but a nointment of wish-wash. He was after givin' her a kind of drug they call a metal wine[1]; but I was afeard, I tell ye, it might send her straight to kingdom come; for they do say that these great doctors kill no end of folks with that same invention.

SGANARELLE, *still holding out his hand and shaking it to show that he wants money*

To the point, my friend, to the point.

---

[1] Emetic wine—the same drug of which Don Juan's Sganarelle tells such marvels. (See Vol. I, pp. 108-9.) Its use had become very popular since 1658, when it had (supposedly) cured the young King Louis XIV. of a serious illness. It was a preparation of antimony. The other mistakes of Thibaut, such as "cordal portions" for "cordial potions," hardly need more explanation than Sganarelle later gives them.

THIBAUT

The point is, Master, that we be come to beg you to tell us what us mun do.

SGANARELLE

I don't understand you at all.

PERRIN

Master, my mother is sick; and here be two crowns we hev brought you to give us some cure.

SGANARELLE

Ah! now *you* I understand. There's a lad that speaks clearly, and expresses himself in proper style. You say your mother is sick of a dropsy; that she's swollen all over her body, that she has a fever, with pains in her legs; and that she is sometimes seized with syncopes and convulsions, that is to say, with fainting fits.

PERRIN

Why yes, Master, 't is just so.

SGANARELLE

I understood your words from the first. You have a father who does not know what he is talking about. Now you want a remedy?

PERRIN

Yes, Master.

SGANARELLE

A remedy to cure her?

PERRIN

That is how we mean.

SGANARELLE

Here, here is a piece of cheese that you must make her take.

PERRIN

Cheese, Master?

SGANARELLE

Yes, 't is a prepared cheese, in which there is mixed gold, coral, pearls, and abundance of other precious things.

PERRIN

Master, we be mortal beholden to you; and we 'll go make her take it presently.

SGANARELLE

Go. If she dies, do not fail to have her buried as handsomely as you can.

SCENE III

JACQUELINE, SGANARELLE; LUCAS, *at the back of the stage*

SGANARELLE

Here comes the handsome nurse. Ah! nurse of my heart, I am overjoyed at this meeting; and the sight of you is the rhubarb, the cassia, and the senna that purge away all melancholy from my soul.

JACQUELINE

Body o' me, Master Doctor, that 's too fine talk for me, I don't understand no word of all your Latin.

SGANARELLE

Fall sick, nurse, I beg you; fall sick, for love of me. 'T would give me all the joy in the world to cure you.

JACQUELINE

Your humble sarvent, sir; I 'd **rather** not hev to be cured.

SGANARELLE

How I pity you, fair nurse, for having such a jealous nuisance of a husband.

JACQUELINE

What can a body do, sir? 'T is a penance for my sins; where the goat is tied, e'en there must she browse.

SGANARELLE

What! such a clodhopper! a man who's always watching you, and won't even let anybody speak to you!

JACQUELINE

Alas! you hev n't seen nothing of it yet; that 's only a small sample of his tantrums.

SGANARELLE

Is it possible? And can a man have so base a soul as to ill-use such a woman as you? Ah! but I know some, fair nurse, and not far away either, who would hold themselves happy to kiss even the tiny tips of your tootsies! Why has fate let a beauty so buxom fall into such hands? a mere brute, a boor, a lout, a numskull . . . Forgive me, nurse, if I speak thus of your husband.

JACQUELINE

Eh, sir! I knows well enough he desarves all those names.

SGANARELLE

Yes, surely, nurse, he deserves them; and what's more, 't would be but his deserts if you put on his head something to punish him for his suspicions.

JACQUELINE

'T is true that if I did n't always mind nothing but his interest, he might drive me to do something queer.

SGANARELLE

On my word, you 'd not do ill to revenge yourself on him with someone.   'T is a man, I tell you, who richly deserves it; and if I were lucky enough, fair nurse, to be chosen to . . . (*At this point, seeing Lucas, who was behind them listening to their conversation, they start aside and go off in opposite directions, the doctor with much comical by-play.*)

SCENE IV

Geronte, Lucas

GERONTE

Oh! Lucas! have n't you seen our doctor here?

LUCAS

'Deed I have, deuce take it, I seen him, and my wife too.

GERONTE

Where can he be then?

LUCAS

I dunno; but I wish he were gone to all the devils.

GERONTE

You go and find out about my daughter.

SCENE V

SGANARELLE, LEANDRE, GERONTE

GERONTE

Ah! sir, I was asking where you were.

SGANARELLE

I had just stopped in your yard to expel the super-fluity of drink.　How is the patient?

GERONTE

A little worse since your medicine.

SGANARELLE

So much the better; 't is a sign it is taking effect.

GERONTE

Yes; but I am afraid that while taking effect it may finish her.

SGANARELLE

Don't worry. I have medicines that make mockery

of all extremities, and I look forward to seeing her at her last gasp.

GERONTE, *pointing to Léandre*

Who is this man you have with you?

SGANARELLE, *making signs to show he is an apothecary*

'T is . . .

GERONTE

What?

SGANARELLE

The one . . .

GERONTE

Eh?

SGANARELLE

Who . . .

GERONTE

I see.

SGANARELLE

Your daughter will need him.

SCENE VI

LUCINDE, GERONTE, LEANDRE, JACQUELINE, SGANARELLE

JACQUELINE

Master, here 's your darter, as wants to walk a bit.

SGANARELLE

'T will do her good. You, Mr. Apothecary, just

go and feel her pulse, so that I may talk with you presently about her ailment. (*At this point he draws Géronte aside to a corner of the stage, and passing one arm over his shoulder, puts his hand under his chin, and so makes him turn around toward himself whenever he tries to see what his daughter and the apothecary are doing together; meanwhile speaking to him as follows, to hold his attention:*) Sir, 't is a great and subtle question among the learned, whether women are easier to cure than men. I beg you to listen to this, please. Some say no, others say yes, and I say both yes and no; inasmuch as the incongruity of the opaque humours which meet together in the natural temperament of woman, being cause that the sensual part is always seeking to gain ascendancy over that which hath sense, we see it result that the variability of their opinions depends upon the oblique movement of the circle of the moon; and since the sun, which darts its rays upon the concavity of the earth, finds . . .

LUCINDE, *to Léandre*

No, I am absolutely incapable of changing my sentiments.

GERONTE

My daughter speaks! O marvellous medicine! O admirable doctor! How deeply obliged to you I am, sir, for this wonderful cure! What can I do for you after such a service?

SGANARELLE, *walking about the stage, and wiping his forehead*

This distemper has cost me a vast deal of pains!

LUCINDE

Yes, father, I have recovered my speech ; but it 's
only to tell you that I shall never have any husband
but Léandre, and that it's useless for you to try to
make me marry Horace.

GERONTE

But . . .

LUCINDE

Nothing can possibly shake my resolve.

GERONTE

What !

LUCINDE

'T will be useless to oppose me with fine arguments.

GERONTE

If . . .

LUCINDE

All your rhetoric will serve no purpose.

GERONTE

I . . .

LUCINDE

'T is a thing on which my mind is made up.

GERONTE

But . . .

LUCINDE

No paternal power can compel me to marry
against my will.

GERONTE

I have . . .

LUCINDE

All your efforts will fail.

GERONTE

It . . .

LUCINDE

My heart can never submit to such tyranny.

GERONTE

There . . .

LUCINDE

And I 'll rather cast myself into a convent than marry a man I do not love.

GERONTE

But . . .

LUCINDE, *fairly shouting*

No. By no manner of means. Not for anything. You are wasting your breath. I 'll do nothing of the sort. That is settled.

GERONTE

Oh! what a torrent of words! There 's no standing up against it. (*To Sganarelle*) Sir, I beseech you to make her dumb again.

SGANARELLE

That is impossible. All I can do for you is to make you deaf, if you like.

GERONTE

Many thanks. (*Turning to Lucinde*) Do you expect . . .

LUCINDE

No. All your arguments will have no effect upon me.

GERONTE

You shall marry Horace this very evening.

LUCINDE

I will marry Death sooner.

SGANARELLE, *to Géronte*

Heavens! Wait a bit : let me medicine the matter ; 't is a disease that is on her, and I know what remedy must be applied.

GERONTE

Can it be, sir, that you are able to cure this distemper of the mind also?

SGANARELLE

Yes ; trust me for it, I have remedies for everything ; and our apothecary will help us with this cure. (*He calls the apothecary.*) A word with you. You see that the passion she has for this Léandre is completely contrary to her father's will ; that there is no time to be lost, that the humours are greatly aggravated, and that we must promptly find out a remedy for the disorder, since it might grow worse with delay. For my part, I can see but one, and that is a dose of purgative flight, which you will mix properly with two drachms of matrimonium in pills. Perhaps she will object to taking this medicine; but as you are a skilful man in your business, 't is for you to bring her to it, and get her to swallow the thing as best you may. Go and make her take a turn in the garden, to prepare the humours, while I hold her father in conversation here; but above all, lose no time. To the remedy, quick! to the specific remedy!

SCENE VII

GERONTE, SGANARELLE

GERONTE

What drugs, sir, are those you have just mentioned? It seems to me I have never heard their names before.

SGANARELLE

Certain drugs which are used in cases of urgent necessity.

GERONTE

Have you ever seen insolence the like of hers?

SGANARELLE

Girls are sometimes a bit headstrong.

GERONTE

You would never believe how infatuated she is with this Léandre.

SGANARELLE

The heat of the blood causes such things in young people.

GERONTE

For my part, from the moment I discovered the violence of this passion, I had the sense to keep my girl shut up.

SGANARELLE

You acted wisely.

GERONTE

I saw to it that they should have no communication with each other.

SGANARELLE

You were right.

GERONTE

Some folly would have come of it, if I had allowed them to see each other.

SGANARELLE

Certainly.

GERONTE

And I think the girl would have been capable of running away with him.

SGANARELLE

You reason like a sage.

GERONTE

I have learned that he is doing his utmost to get speech of her.

SGANARELLE

The rascal!

GERONTE

But he will waste his time.

SGANARELLE

Ay! ay!

GERONTE

I shall take good care he does not see her.

SGANARELLE

'T is no fool he has to do with, and you know a trick or two he kens not of. A man must get up betimes to catch you napping.

SCENE VIII

Lucas, Geronte, Sganarelle

LUCAS

Oh! gadzooks, Master, here 's a fine kettle o' fish! Your darter 's been and run off with her Liander. 'T was he that played the 'pothecary, and there be Master Doctor who done this pretty operation.

GERONTE

What! murder me in this fashion! Here, a constable, and don't let him get out. Ah! traitor, I will make you suffer the law.

LUCAS

Ay, faith, Master Doctor, you shall be hanged; only don't you budge from here.'

---

¹ The joyous hope of Lucas is not altogether unfounded; for in ancient criminal law "abductors and their accomplices" were actually in danger of capital punishment.

SCENE IX

MARTINE, SGANARELLE, LUCAS

MARTINE, *to Lucas*

Oh heavens! what a deal of trouble have I had to find this house! Pray tell me some news of the doctor I sent you to.

LUCAS

Here he be, just a-goin' to be hanged.

MARTINE

What! my husband hanged! Alas! and what has he done to come to that?

LUCAS

He 's been and got our master's darter carried off.

MARTINE

Alas! my dear husband, is it really true that they are going to hang you?

SGANARELLE

You see. Alas!

MARTINE

Must you die, before so many people?

SGANARELLE

What would you have me do?

MARTINE

Ah! if you had but finished a-cutting of our wood, I might take some comfort in it.

SGANARELLE

Begone from here, you break my heart.

MARTINE

No; I will stay to encourage you to die. I will not leave you till I 've seen you hanged.

SGANARELLE

Alas!

SCENE X

GERONTE, SGANARELLE, MARTINE

GERONTE, *to Sganarelle*

The constable will be here presently, and you shall be put in a safe place where they 'll answer to me for you.

SGANARELLE, *on his knees, the high pointed hat in his hand.*

Alas! won't a little cudgelling do instead?

GERONTE

No, no; the law shall take its course. But what do I see?

SCENE XI

GERONTE, LEANDRE, LUCINDE, SGANARELLE, LUCAS, MARTINE

LEANDRE

Sir, I am come to bring Léandre before you, and to give Lucinde back into your power. We had intended to run away together, and be married; but this intention has given place to a more honourable procedure. I would not steal your daughter away from you : 't is from your own hand alone I will receive her. What I would say to you, sir, is that I have just now received letters which inform me that my uncle is dead, and that I am the heir to all his property.

GERONTE [*whose stick was uplifted over Léandre, lowers it and at the same time himself bows low to the ground.*] Sir, your virtue holds an ample place in my esteem, and I give you my daughter with all the joy in the world.

SGANARELLE, *aside*

Medicine has had a close shave !

MARTINE

Since you are not to be hanged, thank me for making you a doctor, for 't is I who got you that honour.

SGANARELLE

Yes ! 't is you who got me no end of cudgelling.

LEANDRE, *to Sganarelle*

The result is too happy for you to harbour any grudge.

SGANARELLE

So be it, then. (*To Martine*) I forgive you those blows, in consideration of the dignity to which you raised me ; but prepare to live henceforth in great respect toward a man of my consequence, and remember that the wrath of a doctor is greatly to be feared.

IRISH FOLK PLAYS

By

LADY GREGORY

First Series. The Tragedies

GRANIA　　　　**KINCORA**　　　　**DERVORGILLA**

Second Series. The Tragic Comedies

THE CANAVANS　　　　**THE WHITE COCKADE**

THE DELIVERER

Lady Gregory has preferred going for her material to the traditional folk-history rather than to the authorized printed versions, and she has been able, in so doing, to make her plays more living. One of these, *Kincora*, telling of Brian Boru, who reigned in the year 1000, evoked such keen local interest that an old farmer travelled from the neighborhood of Kincora to see it acted in Dublin.

The story of *Grania*, on which Lady Gregory has founded one of these plays, was taken entirely from tradition. Grania was a beautiful young woman and was to have been married to Finn, the great leader of the Fenians; but before the marriage, she went away from the bridegroom with his handsome young kinsman, Diarmuid. After many years, when Diarmuid had died (and Finn had a hand in his death), she went back to Finn and became his queen.

Another of Lady Gregory's plays, *The Canavans* dealt with the stormy times of Queen Elizabeth, whose memory is a horror in Ireland second only to that of Cromwell.

The White Cockade is founded on a tradition of King James having escaped from Ireland after the battle of the Boyne in a wine barrel.

The choice of folk history rather than written history gives a freshness of treatment and elasticity of material which made the late J. M. Synge say that "Lady Gregory's method had brought back the possibility of writing historic plays."

All these plays, except *Grania*, which has not yet been staged, have been very successfully performed in Ireland. They are written in the dialect of Kiltartan, which had already become familiar to readers of Lady Gregory's books.

G. P. PUTNAM'S SONS

NEW YORK　　　　　　　　　　　　**LONDON**